# KAITUHI RAWHITI

# KAITUHI RAWHITI

# *A Celebration of East Coast Writers*

*Edited by Aaron Compton,
Christopher McMaster, Gillian
Moon, and Claire Price*

Tairawhiti Writers' Hub

We would like to thank the Margaret King Spencer Trust for their Writer's Encouragement Grant that made publication of this anthology possible

We would also like to acknowledge the members of the Tairāwhiti Writers' Hub, and all writers on, or with a connection to, the East Coast of Te Ika a Maui in Aotearoa/New Zealand

# Contents

**Part 3: That year called 2020**



**Part 4: Graphic Story**



**Part 5: Kaituhi Rangatahi**



**Part 6: Poetry**

## Part 7: Speculative and Science Fiction



## About the Authors     239

# INTRODUCTION

## WITI IHIMAERA

1.

I was trying to think of an image that could accompany this introduction.

Something that would convey the pleasure of reading the work of the seventeen poets, twenty-one prose writers (some doubling as poets in this collection) and one graphic artist who appear in *Kaituhi Rawhiti.*

It's like hanging out with a group of Coasties enjoying a barbecue at the beach. We've just had a feed from the grill of sausages and kai moana, cooked to perfection by the four editors, Aaron Compton, Christopher McMaster, Gillian Moon and Claire Price, our glasses have been filled with either beer or wine (well, for the adults), and now it's time to break out the guitar and sing some songs.

These contributors each sing a mean waiata.

2.

*"I am from*
*summer days of endless writing*
*an ocean's worth of hope."*

So writes Moana Hoogland in her appealing poem *I Am From,* and perhaps I can start my introduction by saying how impressed I was to read nine writers who at the time of publication were school students. Fledgling writing was specially sought out by the editors, and some of the students attended the Gisborne Teen Writers' Hub which is itself an initiative to commend. Apart from Moana's work, the success of the hub is evident in Jacqueline Te Kani-Nankivell's *The Missing Science Partner* (I have come across Jacqueline's work in the Piki Huia Short-Story Writing Awards) and Roman Seaton's *The Wrongs of the Marshlander.* In his biographic notes, Roman says he hopes someday to write a book of his own. Go for it, Roman, along with all your companion kaituhi rangatahi!

You all remind me of my own school writing origins, when Mr Bob Grono, English teacher at Gisborne Boys High in the early 1960s encouraged me to write a story for the end of year school magazine. I won the competition but, frankly, I reckon that nobody else entered. Still, the publication inspired me to dream that I could make it someday, yeah right. I may have been the only boy in it, for all I know. But it started me thinking about a writing career and, after many years, achieving it.

Norman Maclean was another of Bob Grono's students. It's great to see him in *Kaituhi Rawhiti* with his story *Stream of Thought,* a very clever title for a stream of consciousness piece using second person narration and finely tuned imagery:

"Leaves are letters that got lost in the mail, a whole sack full like the contents of a man's heart that fly and drift because it's the river not the wind that snatches them, sends them spinning over small rapids where they become fish, galleys, wingless birds and the whole day goes whoop, whoop, like a boy on a fast bike."

The accumulations of disparate images perfectly matches the delirious sense of movement that flows through this piece of a man by a river reflecting on his life and the people in it.

Reflection, allowing the memory to speak, garnished by good old Gizzy humour, is what propels many of the poems and stories from the more mature voices. As such, most are like pieces of whakapapa, genealogy, that many listeners at our barbecue will enjoy because they can recognise the settings. Surfing at Makorori Beach in Ruth Helmling's *Another Day*. Ruatoria and Mount Hikurangi in Hughie Hughes' *Saving Des*. The Pahikiroa Valley in Alison McKay's close encounter story, *What Did We See?* Katrina Reedy's *Ode to Oneroa*, achieves both personal and cultural insights. What looks at first sight to be a simple narrative of memories of Waikanae Midway, expands to include Māori history, Horouta waka and a reminder that there's a genealogy to acknowledge - that of Hine Hakirirangi, ancestress of our region.

Even the Waioeka Gorge plays a supporting role in Dan Witter's hilarious story, *View From a Fruit Box*. Our ancestors arrived on the East Coast in a variety of ways. Maia on a waka made of gourds. Pourangahua on the back of a giant albatross. Paikea on the back of a whale. But Witter's hero's migration beats them all. This one is told with such a straight face, it's a real Coastie hardcase piece that will have you digging your toes in the sand.

In such stories and poems, the history and geography of the East Coast and Gisborne is worn lightly. The writers might not give such a strength of Tairāwhiti identity as those of our nationally-known writers like Anne Salmond, Noel Hilliard (he boarded at Gisborne Boys High), Haare Williams, Monty Soutar, David Ballantyne, Mere Clark, Keri Kaa and Mere Whaanga, but there is a sufficiency of detail to reflect on, smile about and ground us in the familiar.

Barbara Berge in *The Harrods' Bauble* traverses geographies, London and Gisborne, deploying the image of a small Christmas ornament as a time machine in a story about coming home. And having swum a lot at the Waiherere Domain's pool (late at night with mates and girlfriends, don't tell mum), I particularly responded to Lyra Caughley's evocative *Paint Eternity*. Robyn Owen's *A House on Huxley Road* is an exceptional, nuanced, story; she layers her narrative with detail and character points, building a devastating impact that's bound to stay with you for the rest of the day.

Of course, not all the stories and poems have East Coast or Gisborne settings. Interestingly, twenty-five of the writers are women, which reminds me of the great contribution to New Zealand of women writers like Katherine Mansfield, Janet Frame, Patricia Grace and Margaret Mahy. This is the whakapapa that many of the writers in the collection can look back to. For instance, I can sense a bit of Ngaio Marsh in Dorothy Fletcher's *Diamonds are Forever*. She shows a writer fast on her heels, teasing, full of brio and verve.

And at the other end of the scale there's Gillian Moon's poetry sequence, *Letters from Lockdown,* as well as Claire Price's poem on lockdown. They're as perceptive as any similar sequences or poems by any of our contemporary New Zealand poets.

3.

*"I was born somewhere
Now I do not live there…"*

These are the first two lines in Josiah Goddard's poem, *Home.* They evoke the existential dilemma in the questions who we are, where are we from and who represents us.

They lead me to observe that in an anthology entitled *Kaituhi Rawhiti,* readers might justifiably ask where the Māori voices are. According to Ministry of Health, Tairāwhiti DHB statistics 2018/2019, the number of Māori is 50 per cent of the total Gisborne-East Coast population. Happily, while Māori voices are mainly singing elsewhere through the te reo tradition – articulating their culture and politics within the oral forms of Māori literature and art expressivity – *Kaituhi Rawhiti* reveals that our writers are also engaging with the European artform of written literature in English. I've already referred to Robyn Owen's exceptional story set on Huxley Road; let's all wish her well as she goes forward to writing a novel and autobiography. Katrina Reedy has just completed a Graduate Diploma in Arts: Creative Writing; not only that, she takes a writing hub for Māori so as to provide opportunities for kuia and koroua, as well as others, to write down their memories. Thank you, Katrina. And I have come across Jacqueline Te Kani-Nankivell's work in the Piki Huia Short-Story Writing Awards, which has the indications of creative talent.

Whether the stories and poems are written by Māori or Pākeha, it's terrific to see that the Māori story is not absent from the Tairāwhiti story. After all, we've been intermingling for many years. I was particularly moved by the sense of epic in *Crushed Violet,* a story by R. de Wolf, about a young girl, Violet Kopua with a soldier, Pera Sampson, which begins in 1938 and takes in the Māori Battalion and WWII. Similarly, with Katarina (Kath) Porou's affecting poem *Heemi Te Whatu Apatari (Jim Porou) Reg. no 817740* honouring the Battalion. And Rodney Baker, in *My Sister,* gives us an expressionist poem on a Covid-19 tangihanga, which had me reflecting on how our culture must roll with the punches but always try to right itself on tikanga.

Sarah Holliday Pocock's character Nell, in *Gravel,* gets a bit of whakawhanaungatanga from a woman named Wai, just off some East Coast road, in a story that weaves effortlessly between Pākehā and Māori, Aotearoa and New Zealand. Aaron Compton's *Grow Me Some Wings,* is really, really inventive, and I love that it is grounded in Gizzy.

Then there's Karen Morris-Denby's three assertive poems, *Waka Ama Wahine, Waka Ama Wahine Karakia* and *Haiku* with its:

*"Voices in the wind*
*Whispering along the sands*
*Gisborne's secrets past"*

Such lines remind us that the voice of Te Tairāwhiti is a rich and complex one. It is like the full strum of the guitar at our barbecue sing-along, resonant, inclusive.

Finally, I can't leave the campfire without saying to everyone in this anthology, good job! To your editors, what a terrific stroke of genius to include a section of speculative fiction. Like many other writers, I am going into what some have called Climate Fiction (cli-fi), and two new stories in this vein are appearing in the anthologies *Scorchers* (Five Dog Books) and *Monsters in the Garden* (Victoria University Press). I thought all of the stories in this section by Janine Hamilton-Kells, Christopher McMaster, Claire Price, Aaron Compton and Dorothy Fletcher to be really innovative.

And I want to take my hat off to Mr McMaster. One of the wonderful aspects of reading new work is that you come across someone you've never read before. Mr McMaster's poem *Dead Poets Society* had already impressed me with its literariness, so I had to check out his biographical note. His story *Journey to the Stars* has me very glad that he is a Gisborne writer.


Kia kaha koutou, kia manawanui.

Witi Ihimaera

# PART 1

# STORY

The author Jonathon Gottschall observed that, "We are, as a species, addicted to story. Even when the body goes to sleep, the mind stays up all night, telling itself stories." In this section our addiction is fed, and we are invited into the minds of seven local writers who tell their unique story. We are swept along with the flow of musings of a man reflecting upon his family life, which run parallel with a river he observes whilst on an afternoon outing in *Stream of Thought* by Norman Maclean. Barbara Berge tells of a trinket that becomes a family treasure in *The Harrods Bauble*. In *Gravel*, Sarah Pocock invites us into the intimate space of loss and change when a family member suffers a stroke. We are treated to flash fiction from Karen Morris-Denby in *The Amazon*, an epic battle in very few words. Robyn Owen introduces us to a young girl who only wanted to save the kittens at *A House on Huxley Road*. In the spirit of the classic detective story, Dorothy Fletcher deals with a thief in *Diamonds are Forever*. And R. de Wolf journeys to a time of war, where love blooms, and the heart is not the only casualty, in *Crushed Violet*.

# STREAM OF THOUGHT

*NORMAN MACLEAN*

It swallows everything, this serpentine flow. Lick, lap, swirl: eddies under the opposite bank are the coolest places, those patches of shadow as green-black as an old coat. A whirl, then a ripple, easily lifting that floating leaf that pretends to be a craft making its flimsy voyage right past the rocks at the edge, straight past your feet.

In the shallows, stones are content to lie there forever, it seems. Light flicks over them as the current runs and all that is concealed seems of no account, whereas you – well, you lean out, peering, your eyes damp with the glare of it and your nose becoming moist and yes, Goddamn it, that ache well below the belt meaning you must hobble into the shade for a bit, loosen your buttons, take your ease. It's always been the same, urinating out of doors, ever since being caught and shamed at that Sunday school picnic in 1929 with that shout of outrage when you were discovered, remember? The lady superintendent snapped as you turned away, fumbling. A threat of iced cakes denied you as a punishment for your thoughtless indecency made you blush and slink away with your back turned.

A minor stream now to patter intermittently against the pebbles: ah yes, rivers run but old taps have tubes that clog, valves that falter. A damp Morse code spiels some message in stops and starts completely indecipherable, here by the rush of endless water spilling out of those hills and carrying away everything that falls in. A bit like all the years gone by when you stop to think about it – nothing lasting, everything changing, no part of it permanent, except for memory.

It's quiet by the river despite a distant prattle. The picnic has evidently reached that point where crumbs are brushed from jaws with the flick of a hand and a ball has been kicked but being careful – careful – by the water, the kids blunder and laugh at simply being free to bound and trip and tumble. Yelping in the distance blends well, doesn't it, with the burble of water over worn stones as smooth and slick as the pips of a melon. The water can't spit them out but caresses them. Time is a river without banks. Time, like an ever-rolling stream, that's what we used to sing, wasn't it?

Here in this little stretch in front of you, it flows straight and smooth, powering its way to the sea. When it gets to pour itself into the scoop of the bay, it'll be a thing without identity but that's good it seems – that's best when you think about it, a loss of identity. The rush of it and the exhilaration of its passage so like the speed of a car on some long stretch of road without bends, high-charged, roaring.

Across on the other side, trees bend to kiss the smooth face of the water. They sweep tendrils against its bright surface and the link of foliage and free flow is like all the links of a lifetime. It's like this whenever you stare at it, spring, summer, autumn – they touch you too. Winter must be different though, eh – when the water's rushing and dark, and when it overflows its banks, those trailing branches, stripped bare of other seasons, must bend, flex, follow the current or snap and be swept away, a sludge of flotsam that will come to rest on some distant beach and turn to old bones in the sun.

The breeze picks up, leaves fall. Leaves are letters that got lost in the mail, a whole sack full like the contents of a man's heart that fly and drift because it's the river not the wind that snatches them, sends them spinning over small rapids where they become fish, galleys, wingless birds and the whole day goes whoop, whoop, like a boy on a fast bike. There's anticipation in a river, eh. It's hurrying to its destination but it's waiting too and it's keen – really keen – to see what it'll be like when the flow is slowed, the bay opens to receive it, identity extinguished where the wide estuary is speckled with gulls and the mellow country-side is left far behind. Oh, the smell of those fields it passes and gradually leaves behind; tomatoes and corn being harvested, the dry earth as sweet as an Anzac biscuit dipped in tea.

Nice and neat and clean, that's this place under the trees, all pretty colours and no litter. Grass on this side so short it's like someone comes and clips it when night falls. Up in the branches, birds keep making such a bright racket, jabbing their beaks into the fabric of the afternoon. A river gives being solitary a kind of piquancy because it looks as though it needs to be alone too. In the bright sun with light making doilies on its surface, no one – not even you, slumped with splayed legs and that sagging brim to shade your eyes – can break the completeness of it.

On those rocks at the edge, leaves are pasted like carefully clipped pictures from Nancy's scrapbook, their bright golds and reds so warm you could lick them. When she was gone, what happened to it? There were times when you might have flicked through it and seen her again as a small girl, hunched over it on the carpet. You would have wondered, what if? Hugh's cricket bat went in the fire eventually because you couldn't find any boy or girl who might like to have it and what's the use of keeping stuff like that? Hugh got it for his tenth birthday, didn't he? Out he ran to the back lawn, calling for you to come and bowl. A wooden fruit case sufficed as wickets and you hurled that old tennis ball until your arm ached while he sprinted back and forth, snorting with laughter when you had to drop to your knees if you weren't to be disgraced by failing to retrieve the bloody ball, smacked so hard it shot under rhubarb leaves or disappeared somewhere near the lemon tree where paspalum clumped thick and your nails clawed up dirt when you scrabbled.

Nancy had been mystified that morning by their first cricket game. With her doll tucked firmly under one arm as always and swinging thin legs, Nancy perched in the walnut tree thumb-sucking, never mind Moira's firm admonitions. Every time you had to wildly dash after the blasted ball she'd give a ha-ha crow from her perch but then make you feel better by cheering – hurrah, Dad – if you caught the thing in mid-air and bowled again quickly to crack the apple box, whooping to tell the boy he was out. Weird how small things come back to you out of nowhere.

Far better than the tattered scraps that plaster the stones down here by the water are these leaves you sit on, so crisp when you put your palms down hard, they crunch as briskly as crackers you put out with cheese. Like back in the days when Moira would decide that since it was the festive season it must be time to have friends in for sherry. That sweet stuff that lasted so long, housed in the dark recess of the sideboard cupboard with flower patterned plates for company, inherited tea cups, the good silver that never saw the light of day. Sherry – it must be years since you've seen a bottle of it, brown and viscous, scented like strawberries steeped in cough mixture. Cheers, everyone – cheers! Here's to happy days.

Nancy, or is it Hugh, come jogging along the river bank to see if you're okay only they don't. Their feet thudding on the dry turf is the pounding of your own heart, silly old fool. If anything, they'd be running in the opposite direction. Well, wouldn't they?

Nancy stopped being your little girl when she started tying multi-coloured bands around her head and wearing dresses that looked as if they had been made out of cheesecloth with strings of beads or even seeds, threaded on a nylon strand to go round her neck and large dangling hoops that swung from ears invisible under the mane of hair she dyed a strange sort of copper. Barefoot she was half the time and her eyes half-closed, her lids so heavy she was permanently waking up after a late night. She smelt of herbal oils and talked like one of those American jokers on T.V. who wore striped trousers and shirts open down to their navels and called everyone, "man". Moira said they ought to be ashamed and as for you, miss – you're just as bad, hanging about with young blokes who look like girls – all that long hair. Girls used to know how to behave, keep themselves nice, but these days, not one of them showing a scrap of decency, never mind how well brought up they were.

And Hugh – don't start me. He began so well, getting such good School Certificate passes in maths and physics, he could easily have made it into engineering if he'd put his mind to it, but no. Oh no – not that boy. He took up the guitar and had blokes around after school, out in the shed banging drums and wailing their heads off til all hours and burning those bloody awful joss sticks so that the whole back of the house smelt like an Asian tart shop. Be in a band by all means, you told him, but don't think for one moment it's a career, it's just a hobby, you'll get sick of it eventually and then where will you be? Would he listen? Not Hugh, he always knew better. A motorbike it was next and tearing off to do trips. He always said then he'd give that snigger, like he'd just been funny when there wasn't a thing to laugh at, as Moira pointed out, wagging her head at the front window, watching him in his leather jacket roaring through the gate and slanting his way out onto the street without looking both ways while one of his mates came charging up behind him, eager for some distant destination they never identified beforehand.

You get slowly to your feet, holding onto a low branch for a bit of help, just balancing for a moment, then you pick your way down to the water's edge. Something flashes silver under the surface and when you kneel to look more closely you see that it's a small spanner of all things, as if someone tried to make repairs to who knows what, got sick of the effort and chucked the spanner away in frustration. Such a damned waste – you'd really like to take off shoes and socks, wade in carefully and pick it up but the stones would be a bit slippery and what if you fell? You'd look a dope going back to the cars in wet clothes and there'd be nothing to change into. Someone would be sure to take pity, offer a rug to wrap you in after you'd peeled off your cold, dripping things and you'd have to huddle in the back seat, hoping your cough didn't start up. They'd look at you with resigned glances, murmur among themselves, then it'd be, "Come on children, we'd better think about getting home."

No, it's not as if you need a spanner. Leave it for someone who can add it to a tool box. Of course, Hugh never had anything so permanent. Well, he must have had a spanner – of course he would have – but his gear was never scattered around the floor of the shed with crushed beer cans and butts stubbed out on the concrete. He carried a few tools in a bag on his bike that you'd think were not all that valuable, yet the bag came in with him every evening and he'd carry it out in the morning, as if he was in charge of the crown jewels. All the things that used to keep him up half the night were suddenly disregarded: the drum kit and the electric guitar collected dust and in due course were sold to help finance the purchase of the bike that he vowed would change his life. It did that all right and how. He just never looked back.

But you look now at light dancing on that spanner in the river and it makes you think again of the way a single article will bring memories rushing. Moira comes to mind and the way she would sometimes wander into the shed to stroke the old boots that my Hughie left behind as if his legs were still in them, but in her head they had shrunk to the curving pink limbs she had caressed when he was so small he couldn't even stand, never mind think about boots. You used to tell her off for having a quiet snivel and re-mind her that he hardly ever got in touch, did he? Oh, no – he was too busy making a small fortune working in that Australian mine way north of Perth, that's all we knew, then getting himself involved with some crooked bugger who smuggled parrots on a fishing boat to ports in South East Asia. Moira would wipe her nose on a corner of her apron and say, yes, but he was such a very *good* boy when he was little, wasn't he?

Then there was that girl he got up the duff and a kiddy they never got to meet who was named Karma Moira. When the post-card came with that bit of news, the waterworks were on again, full bore. Moira, well she never stopped telling people she had a granddaughter in Oz who was named after her, would you be-lieve it, and people would say how lovely, can we see a photo? Only there wasn't one, but that was Hugh all over. How many times did you both talk about saving to fly across, to meet the partner and the little girl at last, but by the time you got around to it, wouldn't you just know with Hugh, the pair of them had split up and the Aussie mother took her child off to live on some commune on the Gold Coast? That was that.

The water rushes straight and clear so you shift your gaze from that discarded spanner, not even rusted and you wonder about all the places Hugh got himself to before he rode off on that last trip, out of their lives completely and out of the world too, without a backward glance you can bet. Could have been an engineer, but no, not him. Fumbling for a handkerchief you find there isn't even a tissue in your pocket so there's nothing for it but to do a loud drawback – Moira's not there now to tell you off – hoik hard and spit into the water, watching the small gob get rushed away, a very little bit of you disappearing forever the way things happen.

Back there through the trees the kids are yelling and one of the dads is intervening to check a row before it becomes an outright brawl. There's a bit of howling, some gruffly gentle placating noises then one of the boys is shouting for them all to follow him up to the waterfall so after a while the babble of voices slowly dies away. Sounds like a sensible kid, that one, though from this distance you can't tell which one of them it is and you fall to thinking how much you'd have liked a grandson who sounded like that, all confident and cheerful, a kid you could take fishing – Hugh never liked doing that – and perhaps get him interested in war planes and stuff. It makes you wonder if you ever heard Hugh using the same tones as that boy in command of the others. Funny, you can't even remember what he sounded like when he was at primary school, and of course, by the time he was in his teens it was only grunts and occasionally an outburst with slamming doors while you raged after him then gave up and went off to the pub where, over their pints, your mates could guarantee you that they knew all about that kind of delinquent carry-on. Silly young sods, all they needed was a good kick up the jacksie to straighten them out, but of course that's not allowed nowadays, is it? Drink up and we'll have another then better get back or there'll be hell to pay.

After Hugh was gone you were forever telling yourself it was good that at least there was Nancy who'd make you and her Mum a cuppa if you asked her. Sometimes she'd take it into her head to bring you both breakfast in bed on a Sunday and she'd never forget your birthdays, no matter how dreamy she was, always off in cloud-cuckoo land, she and her scatty friends with their heads in a huddle to whisper then suddenly give a shriek and all rush huddling off to her room with the door firmly shut but not slammed. Later on Nancy got herself that quite good job in Wellington but mixed with the wrong crowd obviously and had a little brush with the law at some stage that Moira insisted should only ever be thought of as a silly mistake and they all make them sooner or later, don't they?

You paid the fine of course – made sure that she did her home detention and were quietly pleased when she met some young joker, though he had been Born Again and didn't want a beer when you offered him one that first time. Before you knew it, Nancy had gone the same way, apparently got herself bitten just as hard by the Holy Ghost so then it was all retreats with her Bible in hand and fearful expectations of the Last Days, it was all prophesied in Revelation. She'd tried to convince her Mum and Dad that when she spoke in tongues she felt as though she was going to explode, she was that happy. It led to joining a choir organised by some people at the Sinai Covenant Fellowship. At least she managed to do a bit of good, going off with a group of willing volunteers to sing to the locals in New Guinea, then tell them how they ought to be living. In the process she learned new things herself, like putting up with insect bites while having to avoid wild-looking jokers who carried machetes and certainly liked a drink.

Funny how much she changed when you stop to think about it. She moved on to the Catholics a few years later, enjoyed arguing with the priest, she said, but really liked the women parishioners who actually ran the whole show, because if you pulled *them* out of the church, as Nancy explained more than once, the entire system would collapse. Books of theological and Biblical criticism were what she had on her gift list, when it came to buying her something for Christmas. She ended up needing glasses, cut her hair real short and having long since discarded the muslin gowns followed by the modest gear approved of by the Sinai lot, started to wear jeans with lace-up boots and jackets she bought from the Trade Aid shop since the commercial world was just a joke and look at the state of the planet. When she and her best friend Ngaire went flatting together, became sort of vegans and started an organic garden, it got a bit harder to really know who she was. You would call in sometimes to offer giving them a hand in building their hen house or Moira would decide it was time to have them over for dinner and agonise about making a meal without meat in it. Nancy would tell Mum not to make a fuss – soup or an omelette would do them just fine and would a few tomatoes be any use to you as they had far too many ripening all at once this summer? Next year – well, who knew what?

You thought things had come to a pretty pass as you pulled up the knot in your tie, struggled into that new suit jacket and went off with Moira to the Elysium Winery for a wedding on the lawn like you wouldn't believe. Under trees strung with white lights, a group of women musicians played and a lady celebrant asked all present to show their support for this very significant step that Nancy and Ngaire were taking that special day. Moira had a little weep so you slipped your hand in hers, knowing how much she had always longed to see their daughter all in white coming down the aisle with a nice young bloke on her arm. Still, there had been some beer as well as bubbly and when you made that speech that Nancy said she really wanted you to give, everyone gave a good clap at the end and Moira said you acquitted yourself pretty well considering.

Moira, Moira ... when she went, nothing was the same, was it? But at least you knew how to cook for yourself and you didn't let the house turn into a sty. Her photo in a good frame still sits on the piano where perhaps she can keep an eye on things like always.

The best thing about rushing water is the calm it brings even when it's noisy. Like the peace to be found in a house where a boy has grown up but then one day leaves when he's called away by the sound of bigger, better things than the comfortable clatter of a kitchen in the evening. On the tongue, this river is like a long, slow lick of a wooden spoon made sweet by stirring some memory of smooth stuff thickening in a blackened pan. The taste of it starts tears but by a river, well, what could be more appropriate.

Time to go; you can see the young granddaughter coming to hurry you along. Thank God she dropped Karma as her known name when she married her Aussie because, as she explained, it's not exactly what you expect the wife of a CEO to be called and besides, she's always liked her grandmother's name and now that they've shifted over this side of the Tasman, it makes sense, doesn't it? Moira in shorts and a coloured vest smiles as she approaches, does a little sort of dance on the spot and holds out her arms as if you've been away for a long time.

# THE HARRODS BAUBLE

BARBARA BERGE

It was Sunday and Derek announced that he was going off to 'examine the inside of his eyelids.' I was tempted to go and have a nap too, before our energetic grandsons arrived with our daughter, their mother, but I wanted to surprise them with the Christmas tree. I only had a couple of hours to set it all up with the decorations and blinking lights.

The tree, one of those artificial ones that we'd bought when we first came to New Zealand, was well past its best before. I had to unpack and assemble it with care, since I knew it would set me to sneezing with the dust and grit it had accumulated over the years. I missed having a real one, but they were messy. It was rare to find one the right size and shape to take all of the decorations we'd gathered – and added to every year. You could buy a special Christmas spray now with a pine fragrance. I wondered if it would smell a bit like toilet disinfectant.

I lifted the boxes of tissue-wrapped decorations down from their shelf in my wardrobe. I couldn't believe it had been almost a year ago that I'd packed them all up. "Seems like there's only two months between Christmases nowadays," had become one of Derek's favourite comments at this time of year, but it didn't seem so far from the truth. How fast time was going.

Derek had been only eighteen, and me a year younger, when we got married. He'd been my first real boyfriend and I his first girlfriend. Lots of cuddling and a bit of naive experimenting on my single bed when Mum was out resulted in me getting pregnant – not in the plan at all.

It was three months before I realised what was happening to me. When Mum found out it was a quick trip to the Registry Office and I suddenly became Mrs Beattie. That's what you did in those days.

We managed to squeeze an old double bed into my bedroom at Mum's and my new husband moved in. I had to abandon my plans to train as a nurse and watched with a sort of fascinated horror as my body swelled, my face and hands became puffy, and my feet refused to fit into my shoes. Derek's dream of going to university to study engineering was replaced with the realities of having a family to support, as he took on an apprenticeship as a mechanic. Money had always been tight, especially since my father (the parish parson) had died five years before. Now being 'poor as church mice' took on a whole new meaning. If it hadn't been for Mum, I'm not sure what we'd have done.


Robbie was born a couple of weeks before Christmas. Somewhat unexpectedly, he brought such joy into all our lives. He was a round, amiable and undemanding little fellow – easy to care for. He didn't seem to need much above the basics – a full tummy, love, warmth, and a clean bottom. He was eighteen months old when I got a part time job in the local school cafeteria. It brought in a bit of much needed extra cash and meant we could give Mum a bit of money for board. I managed to salt a few pounds away now and again. I wanted to treat our little family to a special outing to celebrate Christmas and Robbie's second birthday, something special we couldn't have afforded on Derek's meagre earnings.

I decided on an outing to Harrods, a famous department store in London, that devoted a whole floor to Christmas every year. I used to go with Mum and Dad when I was a little girl. I remember feeling that I'd entered some sort of Aladdin's Cave, everything sparkling and glowing and promising. I was never quite sure what it promised because we could never afford to buy much. I loved it though, as did the hundreds of other boys and girls who visited it, all caught up in a fairy tale. Even though Robbie was only little, I wanted him to see it and I hoped it would bring a bit of much needed magic into Derek's life as well.

Sleet and rain greeted us on the day we'd chosen for our trip. Derek had managed to wangle the afternoon off, with the promise of making up the hours later in the week. We set off into the frigid weather, Mum, Derek, and I bundled up in our best coats. Robbie was so cocooned in blankets only his small pink nose protruded. We had to catch a bus from the end of our street to the train station and then a train to London.

When we got to Knightsbridge, we only had a short walk to get to Harrods. As soon as we arrived there we headed straight for the in-store café for our slap-up lunch. I think it was soup and sandwiches, followed by a Christmas mince tart and a cuppa. We thought it was pretty ritzy. Robbie enjoyed his share, dropping very expensive crumbs onto the Harrod's insignia carpet.

I can still remember the look on Robbie's face when we entered the toy department. He had never seen anything like it in his short life. He didn't know where to look at first, eyes like saucers, his head turning this way and that, trying to take it all in. I wanted to buy him a special birthday/Christmas present, so we watched him carefully to see if something in particular caught his attention. Our quest was answered when he let out a loud squawk and held out his arms, stubby fingers working with ecstasy, in a vain attempt to magnetise a small electric train that was running around and around a short circular track, toward him. It pulled a carriage that was stacked with tiny wooden logs and let out a tiny toot toot now and again. Robbie couldn't take his eyes off it and didn't seem to tire of its repetitive journey.

Of course, we all knew that that was the toy we had to buy him, but when I inquired about the price I was shocked. I would only have enough for our fares home if I bought the toy. That meant I wouldn't be able to afford the one other thing I had hoped to get – a Christmas decoration for our tree at home. Mum and I had made paper chains for it and other glittery creations, using crepe paper and old Christmas cards. We thought it looked very pretty, but I wanted something special to place at the top – its crowning glory. There was nothing for it but to bite the bullet and pay up. I couldn't wait for Christmas Day to see Robbie's little face light up when he saw what Santa had brought him.

Fortunately, we were able to distract Robbie as we moved amongst the displays of toys and decorations that dazzled us all. The thing that impressed us the most though, was the magnificent Christmas tree in the centre of the floor that spread wide boughs in all directions and almost touched the ceiling. The light was muted on this floor, the tree bristled and glistened with coloured balls, baubles, stars, toys and other marvellous treasures.

It was enough just to be there, filled with awe and a good helping of Christmas spirit.

When at last we tore ourselves away, we had to hurry for our train. We found, with relief, some seats that faced each other and enabled us all to sit together. Tired out, Robbie soon fell asleep in Derek's arms. As it was warm in the close confines of the train, I loosened the blankets that swaddled the little fellow so he wouldn't cook.

Derek studied his son's sleeping face and smiled. "Thank you, Becky," he said, "we've had a wonderful time." Mum smiled in agreement.

Then something caught Derek's attention. "What's that he's got there?" he said, staring down at Robbie's hands which I had freed from the covers. They were clasped around some object that glowed blue in the poor light afforded by the train's electric light. I leaned over and gently prised the plump little fingers away from the thing they possessed. I held up an ice-blue, hand blown glass bauble. Glittering silver swirls and stylized snow drops decorated its surface. With its fellows and other delights on the Harrods Christmas tree it would have been just one of hundreds of beautiful items but, by itself, it seemed truly delicate and wonderful. It had obviously attracted our little son, who'd reached out his hand and made it his own.

We told ourselves that, had we realised the theft, we would have quietly returned the stolen object to the tree but here we were, half way back to Byfleet. Thanks to Robbie's little crime, we had our special Christmas decoration for our own tree after all.

Forty-five years later, in the heat of a summer afternoon a world away from England, I unwrapped the precious thing again and hung it in its place of honour at the top of the tree. It had faded of course, all the silver sparkles worn away by time and handling, and so many Christmases. But it still shone blue in the sunlight through the window and reminded me of a special time and a little boy's determination to claim his glittering prize.

It didn't surprise me somehow, when the phone rang and it was Robbie, calling from England. "Hi Mum," he said, "what are you doing?"

"Decorating the Christmas tree," I told him. "Guess what I've just hung at the top of it?"

"What?"

"The Harrods bauble of course," I said.

"Oh, have you still got that old thing? Well Mum, you'd better make some extra mince pies 'cos I've managed to get a flight to New Zealand for Christmas. Milly and I and the kids'll be arriving on Christmas Eve."

There was silence for a moment while this news sunk in, then I let out a loud, "Whoop!"

"What's happening?" Derek demanded, as he wandered in rubbing his eyes.

"Robbie's lot are coming for Christmas," I told him.

"Gonna be a tight squeeze," Derek commented, but he was smiling.

Robbie's voice sounded through the phone. "I'll bring you a new Christmas decoration to replace that old bauble Mum."

"No thanks, Robbie," I said. "Just bring yourselves. We like the old one just fine."

# GRAVEL

SARAH HOLLIDAY POCOCK

In these unmapped, fearful days, I'm drawn to the familiar format of a photo and a caption, life distilled into Instagram posts. The crop tool, the filter, are the only tools I have right now. How can they be enough? They'll have to be.

No one knows this thread is here. It might be good to have it later. Or maybe I'll delete this secret account.

Today I stopped the car on a 100k road, feeling lost in the world, in time, in the script that I thought was our life. I knew what road I was on and how to find my way back. This East Coast city would be a hard place to truly lose yourself. But instead I felt lost in time. I don't know what direction will take us where we're meant to end up.

I stared at the loose gravel.

*What do I do now?*

I turned the corner onto the ward and nodded to the nurse at the station. He smiled and said, "Back so soon?"

"Has it been soon? Time is funny right now."

"He's been resting. He's doing well."

"That's great to hear. I'll go have a peek."

I hooked my finger around the sky blue curtain and peered in. His eyes fluttered open. My heart was a warm, overripe peach, soft and delicate and only just holding itself together.

"Hey," I whispered.

"Hey," he whispered back.

"How are you doing?"

"Good."

"It's quiet here. Did you get some rest?"

"Yes, I must've. What about you? I'm not going to be able to get better if I think you're not taking care of yourself." Typical, how caring and selfless he'd be.

"No, I'm fine. Good." I ask the question I fear the answer to: "Any change?"

"No." He looks down at his left side, paralyzed from the stroke.

Our tween gave this critique of our marriage just a few weeks ago: "You guys are so *boring*!" Our grocery lists and texting the plumber apparently pained her. Maybe I agreed with her? Then it wasn't boring. I clawed the air, trying to grab anything to stop it. But there was nothing to grab. The theatre of our life went silent, and then black. I turned in circles, waiting for our eyes to adjust, to see our way in some new direction. That's where we are now, the two of us, in the black, holding on to each other, hearing our breathing, our attempts to comfort each other.

"What can I get you? Are you comfortable?" I ask.

"I was thinking a shower would do me good."

And that's when a few minutes later, with Brent, the nurse's help, we had Sean in a wheelchair. It involved a hoist, which was horrible. To need a motorised contraption, cradling you in its unfeeling, powerful embrace. It's a cruel realisation. I don't know how Sean is coping.

But after a few moments of fabric sails and hooks, and listening to the groan of the gears, we found ourselves realising the punchline to the joke about attempting modesty in a medical gown. Spoiler alert: it's balls. Sean and I devoured the horrifically immature and yet exquisite jokes. "I feel really bad that Auric is missing this," I said through delicious, weepy laughter referring to our eight-year-old son, whose soul is nourished by all things toilet-related. We laughed more, just at the thought of Auric's infectious laughter.

Finally, Sean was sitting in the 'shower' wheelchair and the fabric of the hoist was lying on the bed, somehow still cocky despite being a folded piece of fabric.

Looking at me, Brent asked, "Are ready to give this a crack?"

"What do you think, Sean? Do you want a medical professional to shower you? Or someone standing near a medical professional?"

"You, if you're up for it," Sean said.

"Okay. Let's do this!" And that's when I steered his wheelchair into a door jamb.

"I'm so sorry!"

"It's okay. I've got 4 other working toes."

I wheeled Sean into the roomy toilet/shower room and locked the door. We learned in that room that, first things first, you need to lock the wheel of the wheelchair.

The second thing we learned is that I should've taken Brent up on the plastic apron.


When I feel profoundly lost, like the world doesn't want to know me, the inside of my car still knows me.

I was in some unspecified moment in the last few days. Sean's condition had stabilized. Tests had been run and calls to the surgeons in Waikato, to family abroad had been made. We'd tried to eat and sleep and be comfortable. I'd sorted our kids with friends and sorted my work. (I never knew "Compassionate Leave" was a thing because I'd never bothered to read The Guide to the Unpleasant Realities of Being an Adult).

On an errand to retrieve items from home, I took a detour on my way back. Waiting for me on a gravelly patch of straight, country road was a spot to sit and ride out this new kind of vertigo.

The kids had been mercifully embraced by friends who were distracting them with some wonderful Kiwi activity. They might've been eeling at that very moment. Eeling ... The image was slick, somehow soothing.

I was grateful for this brief untethering to the kids. I tell myself that our tween daughter and eight-year-old son paint complex and stunning versions of themselves for the rest of the world. But the post-stroke self-portraits they painted for me to see? They were rushed and dissonant. Our daughter veered between mean sass and preacher of Kardashian doctrine. The eight-year-old alternated between sound-effects machine and, this week, author of 'cowboy making love' stories, which thankfully had no actual love-making and fizzled out after the first description of the cowboy's impressive abs. Maybe they were trying to show me more but I just couldn't see it. I was spinning like a toy top, close to the table's edge.

No one is following this Instagram feed so I can say this. What I was really doing in the dusty interior of our old sedan was conjuring the ghost of the boy I loved in college who died the year we all turned thirty. This is something I've done before.

Really, I wanted the other half of my husband back. The half that now embodied all our fear. What if he died? What if he never walked again? Would he never need to buy another pair of massive running shoes that I would trip over? I wanted to be annoyed by those shoes for the rest of my life.

It hurt to want those things. So instead I opted for feeling twenty years old. When the only thing I truly feared was the terrifying edge of whether me and my crush might finally kiss. What a life I've been given.

It's shameful. I know. But I was untethered.

I took shallow breaths. A Ute approached along the relentlessly straight road for what seemed like five minutes. The old guy raised his index finger off the wheel, the Kiwi wave. In the 100 km dust wake that followed the ute, I heard John's voice next to me.

"What are you doing, Nell?" he asked, his voice muted with concern. He always used his nickname for me.

"John." I sighed, soggy with relief. I'd been as dry and cracked as the empty Gisborne sports fields in the dead of summer, but at the sound of his voice, arriving from across decades, geography, the great unknown, I felt the water table in me rise.

My eyes pricked with the first heavy, panicked tears of those strange forty-eight hours.

*You know this is gross, right?*

It's kind of crowded in my lonesome. That's my sister's voice. In casting my inner critic, who better than my only sibling to take the legs out from under me with just a word? Out in the world, she's Natalie. But in my head, she's *Natalia*, never afraid to say hurtful things that I fear are true. I love my sister Natalie. Natalia? I hate that bitch. She has one mode: cunt.

*You pulled over in the hopes you could conjure a dead guy you still have a crush on. You're pathetic.*

Dust mites, as ancient as the upholstery, floated around us, my sad fairy dust. I hoped John couldn't hear her.

But it was working. My longing (gross!) had almost transported me to another time, a chapter of my life when I was a Midwestern Girl at a Big American University in Partytown, USA; that chapter contained no sassy daughters or frightening literature written by eight-year-olds. Or husbands. Or strokes.

I kept my eyes on his young legs, even two decades later afraid to meet his eyes. I focussed instead on his tanned feet in leather flip flops.

"We call them jandals here," I said.

"Pardon?"

"Flip flops. They're called jandals in New Zealand. How fucked is that?" I said through sobs.

"It's okay," he said.

*Barf.*


I sniffed up a quart of tears and snot before turning to look at him, just as he was twenty years ago.

There is an old photo that I pocketed once from somebody's roll of photos. Very few times have I taken something just because I wanted it. But that time my hand knew what my heart refused to know. Despite orbiting each other on a taut string of flirtation, we'd never find ourselves knotted together.

Over the years we stumbled into each other's arms four times and the string reverberated like piano wire, loud and fierce. But the rest of those college days, the string was a cotton thread, that sometimes I wondered if only I could see. So I pocketed the photo that belonged to someone else. It was all I would ever have. He sat there now, just as he was in that photo, his olive skin, youthful and smooth, his hair black and shiny, just long enough to form loose curls around his face.

His eyes met mine and he smiled a wide smile, one he knew would lift my spirits. It hurt to want my husband's stroke to undo itself. It hurt to want our boring, old life to reset. So instead I wanted this.

I met John's eyes and he took in my pain and his eyebrows melted just a bit. "Oh, Nell."

I held the wheel loosely, my shoulders heaving, the confusion of the last two days focusing into a pinpoint of helplessness. He set his hand on my thigh. Even though it was bloodless, it was electrifying just the same.

"I want to go back there. Be twenty again. Have a shitty job that pays for a crappy apartment, and not be ruining anyone's life but my own. To not be letting people down who rely on me."

A truckie drove by and looked in. Gave me the country wave too.

The exhaust from the truck took John with it. I was alone. "Wait, John," I said. Get a grip! "You can fuck right off, Natalia."

"Do you need some help?" A woman's voice carried from across the road. She stood against the post and wire fence in a sleeveless hoodie, leggings and gumboots, one hand a visor over her eyes.

My words hung in the air of my empty car.

(*You are such a weirdo.*) I turned to her and smiled. What a question.

He is getting better. Today he was moved out of the ICU, onto a ward. Which is good. But they wheeled him around in a chair that had a support flap to keep the left side of his torso from sagging and his head from flopping to the left.

"You're on the move again, Sean. Hope that's okay," Brent said as he wheeled Sean's hospital bed down the hall. "Sarah, I need to get him to radiology for a few minutes. Are you happy to wait in his room for maybe twenty minutes? An orderly will bring him back."

"Sure thing. You'll be okay?" I asked Sean.

"I'll be fine. When I get back, will you update me on the kids? Tell me a funny story?"

"I don't know how I'll be able to make anything funny out of Auric trying to communicate with the neighbours' chickens through claps. You know, the universal language of one is yes, two is no?" He laughed. My heart was a new peach again, suspended in the early green of summer, forever young, invincible and fearless. "Okaaay. I'll try to think of something."

I left Sean lying in the bed in the hallway, his monitors beeping, the inflating leg cuffs, hissing and sighing.

"You can make yourself at home here if you'd like." I followed Brent to a black hospital chair next to the open space where Sean would be parked. In the small cabinet on wheels, I put Sean's bag of clothes, his laptop, and the sports magazine that I'd been reading aloud to him to help him fall asleep.

"Hi team," Brent said to the three oldies who lay in their beds.

One of them immediately shh-ed him. "Country Calendar!" was all she said, as admonishment.

"Sorry, Glenys," he said in a quieter voice. "You're going to have another roomie for a bit. "

"What's she in here for? A mental problem?"

"No, Janine. This is your roomie's partner. Her name is Sarah."

"Why is she all wet? Mental problem?"

This struck me as funny. "Sorry," I said quickly. "Mental problems aren't funny. But no, I was trying to give my partner a shower."

"It's nice when they give people with mental problems little jobs to do." I squinted slightly, hoping I could tell if she was joking or sincere. I couldn't tell.

"Janine, you lay back so Dorothy doesn't have to put that intubation tube back in. You didn't like that."

"Oh that Dorothy. She's very bossy."

"You be good."

"I will." I watched her literally bat her eyes. Brent said goodbye and wheeled my husband down the hall.

I stood at the window and stared out at some sky and part of the roof and some massive air ducts. None of it made sense.

"They took my clothes." I turned at the voice of the man who made up our foursome.

"That's because you keep trying to walk," barked Janine. "Your hip is broken, Len! You have to stay put."

"I have to get to my clothes." He flung the sheets off.

"Country Calendar! All of you, shut it!" Glenys yelled.

"Len is trying to leave," I said to Glenys, an effort to explain the situation. She glared at me. "Sorry, I shouldn't have said anything. Do you want more volume?" I handed her the remote. She locked her eyes on mine and raised the volume what seemed like a hundred clicks.

Len grunted as he used the triangle handle dangling above him to pull himself up.

"Lay down, Len!" Janine barked. "You're chocka with pain meds, you nutter. You can't get out of bed!"

"He's not listening." I was a little desperate now, still anchored in my black chair.

"Len!" shouted Janine.

"Shut it!" Glenys said to me. I pointed a small finger at Janine. "It's her," I wanted the finger to say.

I walked over to Len, partly to escape Glenys's wrath. I thought of his brittle bones, kindling ready to snap. "Mr umm, Len? I think you're really better off lying down."

"Baah!" he said. Classic old person. Will I say baah one day? Will Sean?

I was afraid to touch him. Old people are so delicate. I was transfixed by his papery skin.

My words to Len were equally non-contact. "Um, Len, you should, I wouldn't, I think probably – "

"Oh, for the love! The mental problems around here!" said Janine. I watched her fling off her covers, swing her legs off the bed, and snap the pulse monitor off her pointer finger. She took two barefooted stomps away from her bed before feeling the tug of the tube in her nose, just one of the many strands of tubing that webbed them to their beds. She reversed herself, snatched at the wheeled pole that dangled her fluid and started again.

"Len. I can't watch you do this." Slapslapslap. She worked her way to us.

The two of us gently wrestling with Len, that's how Dorothy found us, when her squeaking shoes came to a halt just inside our room. "What's all this?"

We froze, all three of us, and looked over our shoulders at Dorothy. The sound of Country Calendar suddenly deafening, guitar music over the sound of sheep baa-baa-ing. Dorothy looked at us as if this had never happened before.

"This isn't what it looks like," I said to Dorothy.

Lesson learned: Dorothy thinks "helping" should be left to staff.

The lady squinted into the sun. "You all right?"

(*Here we go.*)

"I sure am."

She walked two paces into the road. "Having some kind of car trouble?"

"No, just you know, enjoying the scenery."

We both looked at the post and wire fencing that stretched for miles and the great expanse of blue sky. She stood with the toes of her red bands on the middle white line.

"If you say so."

"I'm sorry if this seems weird. I just pulled over to take a break."

"You're not in some kind of trouble, are you?" she asked, taking a step closer.

"No. Sorry I worried you."

She looked the car over. "You're not having car trouble?"

"Ha. It runs better than it looks. I just pulled over to take a minute to regroup."

"Funny place for you to end up."

"It's peaceful."

"That's one way to put it."

"Are you sure you're not running from something? To be honest, I could use the excitement." She stepped up to the car and leaned against it. It gave slightly under her weight. She had strong looking hands but a softly aging face.

She continued, "How about a little whakawhanaungatanga. Where's your accent from? Canada?"

"Close. I'm from the States. But we live here now." I couldn't look past the image of Sean in the hospital bed. My eyes had more tears to cry.

"Oh dear, oh dear. Here you are running from something and I have to prod until you burst."

"No. You're fine. I'm just a bit fragile. I've had a rocky couple days and it's catching up to me."

"Look. Why don't you come in for a coffee? And you seem like a sturdy lady. (*Ha!* Natalia cackled. *She called you fat!*) I have all these ladder jobs that I've been putting off till I had another set of hands around."

I wiped my eyes. Sean started to doze when I tiptoed out thirty minutes ago. "Thank you so much but I should get going. I have someone I have to see in the hospital."

"Oh dear. Well, rain check then?"

I'm typing this in the dull light emitted from monitors, pumps and the hazy yellow light from the hallway. The tap of the phone keys is drowned out by the layers of hums, beeps and various motors doing things for the body that the various bodies in this room can't do. Sean wears motorised inflating and deflating ankle cuffs that encourage circulation and discourage the dreaded clot. The sound of their robotic breathing has become a strange comfort to me.

I should be asleep. Because Sean is going to wake up any number of times between now and 6:55 am when I'll tiptoe out and back home to the kids and their grandma. But as the ankle cuffs snore into the night, I'm happy I'm writing about that lady today. Some days I'm pulled along as if in a strong river current. You could ask me what I saw along the way and I'd say, "water." So, I'm glad I've written about her. In case I never cross paths with her again.

In a loose stretch of time, I found myself on that same stretch of road. I might find John again.

*(Will you get a grip?!)* Instead, the lady found me.

"I was hoping you'd come back!"

She pointed to a gap in the tree line. "The driveway is a bit overgrown. But you can park your car there to get it off the road if you like."

She gave the car a pat. "Follow me," she said.

(*I like her.*) Me too.

I parked in the driveway. The path was hard to make out with the weeds reaching to our knees. "The drive doesn't get used much. Papatūānuku has reclaimed it. Mother Nature."

"Right. Thank you. I'm still learning."

I followed her in the direction of the house. The timber house seemed as fragile as old Len. But on this summery afternoon, it was cheerful, like Janine when she's flirting with Brent. The sun slanted in, catching the confetti of colour, a happy chaos of flowers.

"It's like an old secret back here! You can't see anything from the road."

"Watch your step. There are little things that I never seem to get around to."

I stepped over a wheelbarrow on its side. Once through the door, I took in the interior. Every surface was worn, soft wood, the satisfying soft rolls of fat on a baby. "Wow! This place is amazing ... actually, I don't know your name."

"Yes, let's get down to connections. My name is Wai. My friends call me Wai Wai."

"Nice to meet you. I'm Sarah. I haven't thought of my nickname in a long time, but I was thinking about it out in the car. A long time ago, a friend called me Nell. I don't think I'd want any-one to use it now."

"It's probably good to outgrow a nickname. Not so lucky for my brother, who we called Undies until he died. That sounds meaner as I say that out loud. Anyway, nice to meet you, Sarah."

The jug began to rumble on the counter.

That's when my phone rang in my pocket. "Sorry, Wai. I should take this. Just in case." I held my breath.

The male voice on the other end asked if I'd left a message a few weeks back about losing a school notebook in Uawa. "Yes! God, that's from a lifetime ago. You have it?" I mumbled out the address. "Yes, I can find my way there! Thank you!"

"Our connection?" Wai Wai said to me. "I just found it."

# THE AMAZON

## KAREN MORRIS-DENBY

When the orders came to travel to the coast, only a small number of soldiers were summoned. She would have liked a full army, but there had been little time to gather them.

She imagined they were galloping through the rough terrain over hills and treacherous tracks around the mountains.

Her duty was to defend the castle that had been abandoned and she knew the enemy was approaching fast.

The moat needed to be deeper but, there was no time to get extra help.

With the resources on hand she placed her soldiers on the East, West, South and North Battlements and hoped they would not succumb to the now fast approaching enemy rising with force in the distance.

If she had gathered more of her troops, they may have managed to build an effective rampart but now it was just a race against time.

The first onslaught came quickly. Some of her soldiers fell, but others were standing bravely. She was unsure of what might come next.

The next wave completely knocked out the South wall and there was nothing she could do.

In the end all her soldiers were lost. She could not compete with the incoming tide which completely engulfed her sandcastle, of which she had been so proud.

# A HOUSE ON HUXLEY ROAD

ROBYN OWEN

I sat in the old yellow wash house, the smell of afterbirth fresh in my nostrils. Beside me, huddled within the pile of sugar sacks that Uncle had left there, sat Pango and her six, brand new kittens.

My eyes were red and my face was blotchy, as Uncle's words continued to ring in my small, four-year-old ears.

"We have enough mouths to feed Moko – those kittens need to go. I'll be throwing them in the drum this afternoon"

Every time I heard his words, my eyes would fill and my lip would tremble. I wasn't allowed to touch the kittens, but I sat as close as I dared, mourning their short life, praying I could keep them. I remembered when Aunty Mere had prayed to God that her baby would live. Everyone was at the hospital, and Aunty was holding my little cousin, crying and praying to God that her baby would survive and grow up to be big and strong like Uncle. That baby was now sitting on Aunty's lap while she was having an unu with Nanny Whatu. So, God must be real, I thought – or at least, he liked Aunty and had listened to her.

I closed my eyes, and prayed hard, just like I'd seen Aunty do. As I prayed, I could hear the kittens whimpering. One of the tabby ones was pawing at the air – stretching out his tiny limbs, reaching for me with his little eyes still sealed shut. I looked around to make sure that no one was around to catch me disobeying Uncle, then I reached out to the kitten and touched his paw. He meowed in response and reached out again to me.

"Hello, kitty," I whispered, "Your name is Socks."

I lifted Socks out of the sacks and placed her in my corduroy brown pinafore. She was tiny and still a bit damp. She was so warm though – radiating heat from her tiny body. I lifted her to my cheek and held her close. I knew there was no way Uncle would let me keep them all – but I also knew that I couldn't let them die. I picked up another kitten and placed it next to Socks in my skirt. This kitten was black and white and snuggled up close next to his brother, meowing plaintively. I stroked their little spines, running my fingers down their little backs and along their tiny tails. Looking at this new kitty, I named her Coco, and snuggled the both of them next to my freckled cheeks. They were so warm I could feel their little hearts all the way through their bodies in both my palms and my cheeks. I loved them so much and wanted them to live.

I carefully placed them back down. Both little bodies immediately snuggled into their mama. I wanted to save them, and I had an idea. I made my way into the house, carefully creeping past the kitchen, and tiptoeing into Uncle's room. On Uncle's bedside table, he had a pewter mug that he always put his change into. I'd often seen Aunty stealing coins from there when she sent us down to the dairy for a bottle of milk and some bread. Sometimes, she'd also give us twenty cents each and we could get some lollies too. Today though, I needed more than twenty cents. I picked out two rolled up $2 notes, and slipped them into my pinafore pockets. I sneaked out the back door, through the garden gate, and onto Huxley Road.

The dairy looked so far away. Normally, I would go down with my cousins - I'd never been by myself. I started walking, my little feet trying not to step on the cracks in the hot concrete. I danced down the hill, stepping in between all the different splits throughout the footpath that was never repaired. I side-stepped the anthills that would form where the cracks would meet, spewing out little black ants in tidy orderly lines.

When I got to the dairy, my  aunty who worked there looked at me over the counter, her smoke hanging out of her mouth. I ignored her and walked straight to the shelves that I'd been to with Uncle only the day before. I picked up the same ties that Uncle had bought to stand his tomatoes up, and took them back to Aunty, placing them on the counter before her.

"Is Uncle still in that garden?"

I nodded – wondering if it was still a lie if I didn't actually say the words. She rang up the ties in the old, creaking till, and stretched out her nicotine stained hand.

"Eighty cents, please."

"Can I have some lollies please, Auntie? And a lemonade ice block?"

Looking at me suspiciously, she took an ice block out of the freezer, and a pre-packed bag of mixed lollies, and placed them next to the ties.

"One dollar and twenty-five cents, please."

I reached into my pockets and handed her one of the crumpled $2 notes. The purple face of the Queen on the note, seemed to be looking at me in disgust. Like she knew that I had stolen Uncle's money and also knew how much trouble I was going to get in. I quickly pushed the note across the table and waited for the change, telling myself that I would put the change, and the $2 note that I hadn't used, back in Uncle's money mug.

I quickly left the dairy and walked across the road to find the spot where my cousins would go smoking. They never got caught there, and I knew that I wouldn't get caught either. I didn't want anyone to see me eating my lollies. I crept under the bushes and huddled into the hollowed-out inside of the evergreen conifer tree. There were cigarette butts everywhere, and I tried to clear a spot to sit. When I had settled myself down, I opened up my ice block. I peeled the blue wrapper down and had a mouthful. It was icy cold, and it slid all the way down my throat. Not wanting to get caught, I quickly took another mouthful, and another, until it was all gone. All that was left was the stickiness all over my little fingers. I pushed the wrapping into a hole where a pile of old smoke packets lay, then opened my lolly packet. I quickly scoffed them all down, one after the other, knowing that I had to get home, before anyone noticed I was gone.

As I stuffed the last lolly in my mouth, I crept out of the tree, and into the bright sunlight, still chewing. I could feel something on the back of my bare legs, and when I looked down, I saw smoke butts were stuck all over me. I brushed them off, checked that I still had the ties, and ran all the way back to Aunty and Uncle's house.

Aunty was still in the kitchen, drinking with Nan, when I got back to the house. Other Aunties were there as well now, and I could hear Uncle in the garage with my older cousins and Koro. They hadn't noticed I was gone, and so I crept back into the wash house and sat next to the kittens again. I thought I should give them another cuddle each before I did what I was going to do. So, I sat there, and gave each of them a name. They were meowing loudly, and as I put the last one back in, I heard someone walking up to the wash house. It was Uncle, and he sat on the step of the laundry and put his big bottle down next to me.

"Don't get attached to them Moko. We can't keep them. They need to go."

I nodded, my eyes filling up again as he said those words. He patted me on the head, and walked off, back to the garage. I could hear him talking to Koro about me.

"Mary's girl is a strange one."

"Not like the rest of us that's for sure – must be her Pakeha side."

"All those bloody drugs her mother was on probably."

I wiped my eyes and pulled one of the sugar sacks out from underneath the kittens. Carefully, I placed each of the kittens into the sack, and walked out of the wash house, to the front of the house. Like so many houses around us, we had a fence with wire netting out the front. I made my way through the garden gate again and placed the bag down in front of the fence. Reaching into my pocket, I pulled out the ties, and unwrapped one off the cardboard.

Then I picked up a kitten, put the tie around his neck, then tied the other end to the fence. I did this with each little kitten, talking to them as I went. Singing the special song my Mama used to sing to me as I tied each knot around each little neck. Lastly, I went to my cousin's car, sitting on the side of the road. Opening the back door, I pulled the handmade sign from the back window.

"For Sale – Enquire Within"

I laid the sign on the browning grass beneath the kittens which were mewing and making funny sounds. Thinking they must be missing their mother, I patted each of their heads, and gave them a kiss, before picking up the sugar sack and taking it back to the wash house. Then I crept back into Uncle's room and put the change back into his money mug.

I felt good. Even though I was sad that I would be losing my kittens, I was happy that other people would love them. I slipped into the hallway and stood at the kitchen door.

"Oi! Is that you Moko?"

I knew Aunty had been drinking, and sometimes she would get angry, so I quietly moved into the kitchen and nodded.

"Are you ear-wigging?"

"No Aunty, I was just coming for a drink of water."

"Well, go and get one then."

I climbed up on the stool and turned on the kitchen tap. The cool water gushed out, and I filled up the chipped mug, and carefully carried it down to the floor. As I raised it to my lips, I heard Uncle's voice. He was swearing and yelling in Māori. He sounded angry. I quickly put the still full cup on the bench and ran to go and hide. He must have found out about the lollies. Maybe Aunty from the dairy rang him? Or maybe my cousins saw me in the Smoking Tree?

As I ran past the table, Nanny caught me.

"Where are you running Moko? What have you done?"

"Nothing!" I cried, realising that Uncle obviously already knew and was going to give me a hiding for stealing his money.

At this point, Uncle stormed into the kitchen, holding one of the kittens, limp in his hand, along with an empty sugar sack.

"What the fuck is this?!" he roared, shaking the kitten in my face. "Fucking cat murderer! I always knew you were fucking strange!"

He picked me up in his other hand and took me to the fence. Some of the kittens were still struggling but at least two were just lying there, limp. He shoved the kitten he was still holding roughly into the sugar sack.

"There!" he spat, "You take the rest off, and put them in there too!"

I looked around frantically for my sign – but it was nowhere to be seen.

'But I'm selling them!" I cried, "Someone might buy them Uncle!"

"Who the fuck wants to buy a dead cat, you fucking moron?!"

I was crying, just as much from the continual slaps over my little head as I was for the dead kittens in front of me. Each time I took a kitten off the fence I would get another slap over each ear. By the time I'd reached the last kitten, my ears were ringing and my cheeks were stinging. Uncle marched me to the end of the garden and lifted the lid off a big forty-gallon drum. It was full of stagnant water, green with algae. Picking up a nearby rock, he placed that in the sugar sack as well, then tied a knot in it. Lifting it up high above the murky water, he then dropped the sack into the drum, and turned to tower above my little frame.

"Don't you ever do that again!" he barked.

He was so close to my scared face that the spittle from his tongue flung into my eyes and blinded me momentarily. He slapped me over the head one last time, knocking me to the ground. Then he strode off back to the garage, only stopping to pick up the big brown bottle off the top of his Holden Kingswood. As I lay there, I heard my cousins laughing about what a weird kid I was and Uncle agreeing.

Nobody came to find me. I lay there crying, wishing my Mum would come, and wondering where my little brothers were. Finally, when the stars started to prick the inky sky, I crept into the house and made my way to my cousins' bed. I crawled under the orange candlewick bedspread. I could have gone with the kittens to be in Heaven with them. Then, as I could hear my Uncle singing in the garage and my cousin playing the guitar, I felt

Pango slink onto the bed with me. She snuggled into my little body, and I felt her whimper as I did, crying for our lost babies. I drifted off to sleep with her wet nose snuggled against my clenched fists.

# DIAMONDS ARE FOREVER

DOROTHY FLETCHER

It was a few days before Christmas and I was lazing in the azure waters of a Fijian hotel pool.

I'd been here for a week and nothing had happened. I should be at home getting ready for the festivities.

But why? It was cold, dark, wet and miserable in England. The streets would be full of last minute shoppers, frantic to find the right gift that would be opened in haste and then consigned to a cupboard until it could be recycled as a gift for some other unfortunate recipient.

Christmas was for small children and families. I had neither. I had a beautiful home, more money than I could spend in several lifetimes, a few reasonably close friends and the odd distant relative. If Peter was still with me or we'd had children that would be different. I'd always dreamed of a Christmas surrounded by family and . . .

"Hello," the male voice broke into my thoughts. I looked up and saw a bronzed face framed by thick, white hair smiling at me from the other side of the pool. "Lovely here, isn't it?"

I smiled back. I recognised his face from some photos Charlie had shown me. Maybe life was looking up.

"Beautiful. Better than freezing back home."

"Ah, from the accent you're from England," he said, and then swam over to me. "I'm from New Zealand. Even though it's the beginning of summer there, it isn't this hot yet."

"New Zealand. I've always fancied visiting that country. Might get around to it one day."

"You should stop off before you go home. Have Christmas on the beach."

"Mmm. Maybe."

"Are you going to the do tonight?"

"Couldn't miss an island feast and fire walking. How about you?"

"Course. I'll see you there." He held out a hand. "Brian, Brian Jarvis."

I clasped his hand and shook it. "Sarah," I said, "Sarah Mainwaring."

He turned my hand over and kissed it. "Until tonight."

He let go of my hand, swam over to the steps and climbed out of the pool – not a bad body for someone his age. I could still appreciate good looks. Peter had always said, "Anyone can look and enjoy the view, as long as you don't go tramping over it."

The evening was warm and the air sweet with the scent of frangipani. The torches on the beach flamed against the absolute black of the tropical night, while the gentle waves sloughed as they lapped onto the shore.

A waitress made her way over to me, her hips swaying to the rhythm of the sea. She gently eased a lei over my shoulders and gave me a single frangipani flower.

She smiled. "Wear the flower over your right ear if you are seeking romance and over your left if you are lucky enough to have already achieved that goal."

I had achieved that goal but that was in the past. Which ear was it to be?

I put the flower over my left ear. Maybe I would seek another relationship one day – but not yet.

"So, you have a true love," I recognised Brian's voice coming from behind me.

I turned to face the man I'd met earlier. "Unfortunately, it's the past tense. My husband died nearly eight years ago."

"Terribly sorry," he muttered. I saw his eyes stray to the necklace that adorned my décolletage. "Incredible. I've never seen diamonds as bright as those. They pick up the flames from the torches as if the light flashes from within them."

"My late husband, Peter, was a master jeweller. He created the piece." I flicked my earrings. "He made these too."

He moved his hand towards my ear. "Do you mind?" I turned my head so that he could see the earring. "Magnificent," he whispered.

His warm breath caressed my face and stirred senses I'd thought were long since dead.

"Is there anything I can get for Madam?" A voice came from the other side of me.

I pulled away from the close encounter and turned to face the speaker. It was Charlie, dressed up as an antiquated waiter. It took all my will power to keep my face straight. "May I suggest a pineapple daiquiri, speciality of the hotel?"

"I think I'd prefer the fruit punch, please," I said, knowing I needed to keep a clear head if tonight was going to be a success.

"Bring me a double whiskey on the rocks," Brian ordered.

He took my hand and led me to a table by the pool. It was set for dinner with candles flickering in the slight tropical breeze.

Brian wined and dined me. He flirted and teased, but his eyes often strayed to the necklace and earrings. I was used to this as Peter had been able to bring out the glory in even quite ordinary diamonds. With diamonds as good as the ones I was wearing, his pieces were truly breath taking. His jewellery adorned the rich and famous around the world, even some royalty. But he had valued his privacy and few people had known the man behind the creations.

A hand touched mine, halting my private thoughts.

"Would you like to dance?" Brian asked. Alcohol with an overlay of lust clouded his eyes.

"That would be lovely," I said, and he whisked me onto the small dance floor.

The music was slow and the drum beat was sensuous, almost animal in its intensity. Brian held me close and whispered all sorts of nonsense as we moved across the wooden floor specially laid on the beach for this evening. He gently took my earlobe into his mouth and caressed it with his tongue.

When the music stopped, I pulled back and shook my head slightly to ensure I could still feel my earring touching my neck.

"Thank you for a lovely evening," I said. "Since I have been here, I find the tropical air lulls me towards an early retirement each night."

His eyes lit up. "I agree. Let me escort you to your room."

We chatted politely as we made our way through the hotel, but when we reached my door he pulled me into an insistent kiss, his tongue seeking entry but I kept it firmly at bay.

"Where would Madam like me to put this?" I escaped from the embrace and there was Charlie with his deadpan waiter's face, staring at the wall beyond Brian and I. On his out turned hand he was holding a silver tray with fruit and a small bottle of orange juice. "I believe Madam has an early plane in the morning. The taxi is ordered."

"Thank you," I said as I swiped my room card. "Please put the tray on the table." I turned to Brian. "Thank you again for a lovely evening." I swung the necklace around. "Could you undo the clasp? I have trouble seeing to undo it myself."

I felt him manoeuvring the clasp and I caught the necklace as it was finally freed.

"May I?" he asked, holding out a hand. While he examined the necklace, I slipped off the earrings. "Truly incredible. Your late husband was a genius."

"Yes, he was." I agreed as he gave the necklace back. "Goodnight."

As Charlie walked past us to leave the room, I slipped a tip into his pocket. "Thank you, waiter."

He nodded and left, following Brian down the corridor towards the lifts.

Later, as I lay in bed my thoughts turned again to Peter. He was the love of my life. We had been happy, most of the time. In the early years our hearts had broken when we found we were not able to have children and neither of us wanted to adopt. But that pain had dulled as Peter became my all and I became his. Then Peter had died. Peter my rock, my best friend, my husband, was dead. It had been so devastatingly sudden that I felt that the Earth must stop spinning and the sun never rise again.

But life had gone on, one terrible day after another.

Over the months life slowly took on some form of normality. It had taken seven long years, though, before I had the courage to admit that I needed some direction, some purpose to life. I also needed companionship. Life had to have some spark in it.

A breeze gently teased at my face bringing me back to the present. I knew I had closed the windows and the door to the terrace.

He was here.

I tightened my grip on the rather illegal Taser I had clutched in my hand. I hoped that if it came to it I could defend my honour without seriously injuring myself in the process. I began to think the Taser was a really bad idea.

Sadly, for my ego, my honour was not in danger, only my jewels. What a cheek, but I guessed at my age that was to be expected.

Stealthy footfalls sounded across the bedroom. The wardrobe door slid open and I heard some quiet metallic sounds. I guessed the safe was being opened. A narrow torch beam briefly flicked on, then was extinguished. The footsteps backtracked to the terrace door. A few seconds later there was only the sound of waves gently lapping on the shore.

Suddenly, lights came on outside. There were shouts and stern voices. When the lights went off shortly after, peace reigned again.

My phone beeped – a text had come through. *All is safely gathered in.* I smiled, carefully stored the Taser in its box, turned over and settled to sleep.


The waiter from the hotel was grinning like a Cheshire cat as he strode through the first class lounge at the airport. Charlie the waiter, alias Detective Inspector Charles Longburn, alias the right honourable Charles Longburn, one of the richest men in the country, bestowed a quick peck on my cheek and sat beside me on the well-stuffed leather sofa.

"This is the only way to travel," he said. "You don't mind my being seated next to you on the plane?"

"Not at all. It's a long flight and I'd appreciate the company."

"You are marvellous, you know." He helped himself to a wine from the tray a waiter proffered. "You help us nab them every time."

"Is he on the plane, too?"

"Yes. Back in cattle class firmly handcuffed to two burley coppers."

"He's not going to advertise how he was caught?"

"Nah. Like all the others we've got this year – too embarrassed at being caught stealing fakes. He just wants to keep it all as quiet as possible." He fumbled in his pocket. "Here's the real ones before I forget."

I stowed away the 'tip' I'd slid into his pocket back in my hotel room.

He chuckled. "How did he not know they were fakes he was stealing?" A very good question. "Someone with his skills should know they were not the real thing in the safe."

"It's simple," I answered. "My Peter always said that when someone has seen the real diamonds once, examined them carefully, and ascertained their authenticity, they don't really scrutinize them again, accepting the cubic zirconia as real from there on. Peter always made an exact copy of all the expensive items but with fake stones. Wear the real ones once, people accept the fakes as real the next time. Helps with the insurance premiums if the real stuff doesn't come out too often."

A stewardess came up and put a lei around each of our necks and then handed me a single frangipani flower. I rolled the stem between my fingers.

"Are you really going back to Christmas on your own?" he asked. "You know you'd be welcome at my place. The family's a bit screwy – all my cling-on relatives wandering around the baronial hall, eating to overload, drinking the cellar dry and riding out like lunatics on Boxing Day." He stopped and stared at his glass. "I would really like you to come."

I looked at my flower, then carefully slid it behind my right ear.

"I would really like to come. After all, Christmas is all about screwy distant relations. They can't stay forever."

His smile deepened as he saw the frangipani flower. He slid his arms around me and drew me into a kiss. I didn't resist in any way.

As I lost myself in his embrace, I heard Peter's voice. "Promise me that if I go first you will not spend your life uselessly in mourning. Live life to the full, and if you are lucky enough to have another chance at love, seize it."

It seemed I could be keeping the promise I'd made that day.

# CRUSHED VIOLET

R. DE WOLF

Violet held her mother's looking glass close to her face. She examined herself critically. Turned her head this way and that. Practicing a smile, she touched her hair and pouted her lips. Overcome with frustration, she gave in to the urge to poke her tongue out and make a face at herself.

"Very grown up, Violet," the brown-eyed girl in the mirror teased.

Tonight, Violet would be attending her first dance in town: the New Year's Eve Ball! She would be chaperoned by older sister Frances and her husband Morehu. Papa had been reluctant to let Violet go. Mama's subtle powers of persuasion, however, had triumphed. Violet admired how her mother got her way with Papa. She made him laugh until his whole face softened, his eyes smiled and voila! As if by magic, he agreed.

"Now darling, you have to remember it is 1938, not 1908. By Violet's age we were already married and expecting our first child. She's seventeen years old. I think it would be a shame if Violet turned into an old spinster, don't you?" Mama smiled sweetly.

The matter was settled. Violet was beyond excited. She panicked. What on earth was she going to wear? Could she wear lipstick? Who else was going? Would she know anyone besides her family? Life on the farm was both isolated and sheltered.

The farm provided for the family. They were not wealthy but they were happy. Violet missed her older brother Bill. He had won a scholarship to study at the University of New Zealand in the South Island. Papa now relied on Violet to help with the farm and household chores. Violet didn't mind. Whether it was lambing, making hay, milking the cow or mustering, she loved it. With the others gone, she felt more relaxed about being Papa's favourite. Maybe Papa's affection was the reason she had only attended chaperoned school dances. Now she was going to meet new people, including boys. The thought sent little shivers of excitement through her. Perhaps she would meet a potential beau or be swept off her feet.

"Violet, we need to make you a new dress for the ball," announced Mama in November.

Divine, expensive, fabric was Violet's most treasured gift last birthday. Mama had promised they would make something fabulous, when an occasion arose.

She suspected Mama intended for her to attend the ball all along. Mama borrowed a magazine from a friend who worked at Smith & Caughey so they could choose a style for Violet's dress. They wouldn't need to buy a pattern. Cutting her own patterns was a skill of Mama's, along with whizzing up creations on her Singer sewing machine. Frances was often envied when she stepped out wearing Mama's fashionable designs.

Finally, Violet stood sheathed in the glamorous evening dress. She couldn't believe it was hers. The dusky-rose, silken fabric caressed her skin where the sleeves draped to just above her elbows. The v-neckline highlighted her smooth olive skin. The dress narrowed, with perfect tucks under her breasts. It hugged her slim torso and tiny waist in a perfect fit. Between manual chores and the Great Depression, most women were now fashionably svelte.

The dress was a dancer's dream. Movie stars wore such outfits on posters advertising their latest films. The finishing flourish, was the antique-gold embroidery Mama stitched around the sleeves and neckline. Simple, elegant and gorgeous, Violet loved her dress. To complete the outfit, Frances had lent her gold sandals and she borrowed Mama's golden evening bag – a honeymoon gift from Grandma, decorated with seed pearls. Her lips pouted with Mama's Summer Rose lipstick. They hadn't told Papa about the lipstick, relying on the overall effect to invoke misty-eyed pride. A lace shawl Nana Violet had given her, completed the ensemble. Morehu drove an Austin 10 truck for work so he and Frances were both Fairy Godmother and pumpkin coach until midnight.

Violet looked stunning. Papa blinked back tears as she pirouetted into the room, dress swirling prettily around her legs. Hand raised to her brow, mouth drawn in a helpless moue, she struck her best actress pose. Papa's throaty laugh proved Mama's trick worked for her too. The familiar crunch of the Austin's tyres on the driveway heralded her coach's arrival. Frances burst into the room, exuberant and fizzing. She cooed over Violet's dress, making her turn in circles.

"You look beautiful, Violet. Nobody told me I would be escorting the two most beautiful girls on the East Coast to the dance." Morehu widened his eyes in mock terror. "How am I supposed to keep an eye on both of you?"

Violet purred under his praise. Normally, he pulled her pigtails and told her that she smelled of eau de poo farm perfume. Morehu cleared his throat.

"Frances and I have some wonderful news. We are expecting a baby in late May." The family descended into a shambolic round of hugging, patting Frances' flat belly, hand shaking and shrieking. Mama scrambled to pour glasses of sherry to celebrate the momentous event.

The ever-resourceful Morehu had also arranged to have a photograph taken prior to the dance to commemorate the occasion of announcing the impending birth. He hustled the girls to make the allocated time slot. They rode their jubilant mood to the dance. Violet entranced the photographer with her comic and dramatic poses. He took several photographs before asking Violet to sit for one on her own, free of charge for her. The photographer kissed Violet's hand chivalrously.

"Douglas, Douglas McKenzie, at your service and hoping you will save me a dance?" Violet was momentarily stunned, plus Frances still had her dance card. However, her good manners took over.

"I should be delighted, Mr McKenzie, Douglas," she smiled. People were queueing for photographs now so he reluctantly relinquished her hand to return to work.

Violet made a surprised face at Frances who laughed, took her arm and led her into the hall. She drank in the festive decorations, the buzz of conversation, the music, people laughing and dancing. The buffet looked scrumptious. She pinched herself to ensure she was awake. Morehu took Frances in his arms. They swayed to the music, so obviously in love.

"Please go and dance lovebirds, before I vomit in my purse," said Violet in her snobbiest voice. They looked worried. Violet shooed them away.

"I will be perfectly fine. More likely to meet someone if I am not a third wheel, so scoot." Violet turned her back to them. She tapped her foot in time to the music and studiously watched the band. Frances and Morehu twirled onto the dance floor. They stayed close enough to keep a watchful eye on Violet.

"I can't believe anyone would leave such a pretty girl alone in that dress. It must be my lucky day." The warm male voice came from behind. She pivoted and locked eyes with the most handsome man she had ever seen. Violet's heart slid into her sandals as she candidly appraised him. It gave her time to relocate her voice and composure. His banter stalled in his throat. This goddess had punched the air from his lungs. His self-confidence faltered as they stared at one another.

"Where are my manners? My name is Pera, Pera Sampson. Can I fetch you a drink?" He stammered the words out in a rush.

"That would be wonderful. My name is Miss Kopua, but you may call me Violet," she replied in her best Olivia de Havilland voice. An amused grin lit up her face and Pera's stomach performed gymnastics in response.

"Perhaps you should come with me. Wouldn't want anyone to steal you away before I returned." Pera held out his arm. She linked her arm with his, feeling a ripple of awareness where their skin touched. Violet threw a look at Frances, gesturing she was getting a drink. Morehu turned to wink his approval at her.

"My sister Frances and her husband Morehu. We came to the dance together."

"I know Morehu. We played rugby together and we both attended the same boarding school. The selfish, heartless beast! He could have introduced us sooner."

Violet tried to suppress a laugh, but it bubbled free from her lips. Pera watched Violet laughing, completely smitten. This was the girl he wanted to marry. The revelation shocked him as he hadn't dreamed of settling down, until now. Pera filled a cup of punch for Violet, got a beer for himself while he tried to herd his scattered thoughts and slow his runaway pulse. Violet wasn't faring much better. She wanted to talk to him all night. Dance with him, be close to him and heaven help her, she wanted to kiss him. The cupid's bow curve of his lips as he spoke captivated her. Violet was rescued from her dilemma by his intense hazel eyes, sharp wit and melodious voice.

"Let's find some seats, Violet."

They sipped their drinks, talked, laughed, and ate. A private universe swallowed them whole.

"Do you sing, Pera?"

"I love to sing. How about you? Oh, and would you like to dance?"

"I sing badly when I milk the cow, I play the piano, and I thought you would never ask." Cheekily, she held out her hand to be kissed. When Pera pulled her into his arms, she wanted to stay there forever. The one dance became several dances in succession. Their bodies moved to the music and they inched closer until their cheeks touched.

Violet spied Frances beckoning her to come and get a drink. Violet whispered in Pera's ear and steered them toward her sister. Morehu arrived with drinks for them. Pumping Pera's hand, they shared a traditional Māori hongi in greeting. Pera kissed Frances on each cheek. They had met before, at rugby games and dances. Frances had pale skin, light brown hair and the sister's shared similar features. Violet possessed the exotic beauty of an Arabian Nights princess or Pania of the Reef. They were both attractive, but Violet was heartbreakingly beautiful. As the thought crossed

Pera's mind, Douglas the photographer swooped in and pulled Violet to the dance floor. She mouthed "sorry" at Pera over Douglas' shoulder. A stab of loss lanced Pera, but after just one dance, Douglas dutifully returned Violet to his side.

"Sorry, old boy. Didn't realise she was taken as she arrived alone. You are one lucky man." Douglas looked crestfallen but bowed politely before leaving.

Pera raised his eyebrows at Violet and she blushed.

"I told Douglas you are my boyfriend. I wanted to curb his enthusiastic attention kindly. He was a complete gentleman, but I want to spend my time with you."

Pera's heart soared with hope. Could Violet's feelings be as overwhelming as his? The band struck up a Perry Como song, so both couples hit the dance floor. The night flew by too quickly for Violet. They counted in the New Year. Horns blew, confetti rained down and Pera kissed her. As he brought his lips to hers, Violet closed her eyes. Could she be in heaven? When she opened them, Pera was wearing the same look Papa did when he looked at Mama. Her heart butterflies fluttered as people cheered around them. Frances and Morehu were still kissing, but as they were married, Violet supposed it was acceptable. She, on the other hand, came to the dance alone.

"I hope you don't think I'm forward. I've never kissed a man before. Let alone somebody I just met," she babbled self-consciously.

"Nonsense, Violet," he said. "I think kissing is perfectly acceptable between boyfriend and girlfriend. Besides, I am going to convince you to marry me one day, so I think it's only fair you let me kiss you again." He laughed, kissing her many times until Frances and Morehu came to collect her. Pera and Violet's cloud scudded across the carpark to the coach.

"May I call on you, Violet? Take you to the pictures next Friday?"

"I would love that. I will ask my parents," said Violet.

"I will get your address from Morehu and ask your parents in advance." Pera kissed her hand and almost skipped to his father's Buick.

Mama was awake at home, waiting. Violet was bursting with details. Mama was treated to an effusive gush of information, featuring Pera's every word and expression, until 2.30 am.

The days passed in a haze of happiness for Violet and Pera. They were always together. A milkshake, picnic, swim, hay-making or taking Violet to meet his family. Any excuse would do. Pera's family owned a huge sheep and cattle station and they were delighted to meet Violet. Pera's six younger siblings were curious, especially his four sisters. Violet was intimidated by their large house and flash car at first, but they were so welcoming she soon felt at home.

Unfortunately, Pera had to return to his studies. The young couple knew they would be separated. They promised to write one another and swore they would spend the rest of their lives together once Pera graduated.

When Pera returned home for the mid-year break, all he wanted was to see Violet. They spent each day together and attended every dance in the district. They avoided sleep, staying out late, but time flashed by. The days evaporated in bliss until the holidays were almost over.

Pera got down on one knee.

"I love you Violet, and I can't wait any longer. Will you marry me?" He produced a velvet ring box from his pocket.

Violet jumped up and down and squealed her excitement shouting, "Yes, yes, yes, I'd love to!"

Papa gave Pera his permission and blessing, without hesitation. The ring was Pera's grandmother's. A square cut ruby flanked on each side by three diamonds. Violet adored it and as Pera slipped the ring onto her finger, happiness burst its dam inside her. They decided to marry in the spring of 1940.

Papa called the family into the sitting room. With a serious face, he turned on the wireless so they could listen to the news. Hitler and his Nazis had invaded Poland so Great Britain, along with France, declared war on Germany. World War II began, and although they were in New Zealand, their whole life was about to change.

"What does this mean for New Zealand and us Papa?" Violet looked at her father with a frown.

"Well, we are allied with the British Empire, Violet, so no doubt they will ask us to join them in this war. There will be hard times again. Probably shortages of food, goods and many lives lost again. Weighty but not happy news, I'm afraid," said Papa shaking his head.

"Will you have to go and fight this time Papa?"

"I doubt it. I was wounded in the Great War and I am getting a little long in the tooth. With food in short supply, farmers will need to be as productive as possible I imagine. Unless they become extremely desperate, old codgers like me will mind the fort at home." Papa smiled, trying to lighten the mood.

Violet's father became more concerned when Sir Apirana Ngata announced in October a Māori Battalion would be formed. "The price of citizenship," he called it. Pera's father William was a friend and great admirer of Ngata so it was inevitable his son would enlist. Violet also worried about Bill. She knew he devoured every comment and speech Ngata made. He and Pera shared a healthy interest in politics. Sir Apirana Ngata was a man they both admired.

When Pera next came to see Violet, he was wearing his military uniform. As Papa predicted, he had enlisted as soon as the announcement was made. Violet was excited to see Pera, but when she saw him in uniform, unwanted tears welled. The thought of finding love, then being separated for months with oceans between them, constricted her chest. She wiped her tears, ran into Pera's arms and hugged him fiercely. If only time would freeze now.

"What's with the tears, Violet," he teased.

"You look so handsome as a soldier. I can't bear the thought of other girls looking at you." She pouted her displeasure at the thought.

"There is only one girl I want, and you know very well it is you, Violet." When he smiled it brought out the sun in her world.

"Besides, give us a few months and we will teach those Nazis a lesson. We will send them packing back to Germany with their tails between their legs."

Pera hoped his confident bravado would cheer her up. Violet forced a smile. A weepy, wet blanket wasn't what Pera needed when he was being so brave. They had precious time together.

The new Māori Battalion recruits would be trained in Trentham for a few months so Pera reassured Violet he wasn't leaving immediately. They clung to each other desperately as the future blurred.

It was a subdued Christmas in 1939, with the spectre of World War II casting a long shadow over the globe.

Denmark and Norway were invaded. Pera was granted leave to visit his family but he rushed to Violet's side.

"My darling, do you think we should postpone our wedding until I come home? I am desperate to marry you but you deserve a proper wedding with a dress, honeymoon and – well, a husband."

"I will wait for you Pera. I want to be your wife properly and I will pray you return to me swiftly."

Violet knew she must squeeze every drop of pleasure, from each moment they remained together.

The 2nd Echelon of the Māori Battalion shipped out in May 1940. Pera sailed into war and the unknown. Violet's heart and dreams left with him.

Pera wrote Violet letters from Scotland, Greece, Egypt and increasingly exotic sounding places in North Africa. For her part, Violet wrote about daily life on the farm and the amusing antics of his siblings when she visited his family on Sundays. Violet anchored Pera to her world with her words. The letters also conveyed the depth of Violet's love for him.

Pera had now been gone for two years and Violet could tell from his letters, the war was taxing his soul. Papa had warned her of the harsh realities, the horrors he would face. She worried about Pera and Bill incessantly. Mama did not tolerate her wallowing in self-pity.

"Our brave soldiers deserve better than hollow-eyed, bony girls they do not recognise when they come home."

Violet knew Mama was right.

Petrol rationing had started in 1940. Sugar and stocking rations followed suit in 1942. Many imported goods were no longer available. The country's resources were being deployed to support Great Britain and America in the war effort. Violet and Papa toiled on the farm to produce as much meat and wool as possible. The months dragged on in dreary succession. Life in the farming community trudged on as the vibrant colours of their existence faded, like an old photograph, into a bland sepia. The simple enjoyments they had once shared, and thrived on, leached slowly from their lives. Dour folk went mechanically about their business as they fretted for loved ones. All ladies-in-waiting, to the end of the war.

Violet watched the unfamiliar car approaching. A column of dust plumed misery in its wake. It hung, choking the afternoon air. The unseen archer whipped an arrow from the quiver. Nocked it. The bow was drawn taut, aimed at Violet. Colour drained from her stricken face. Her heart splintered. The earth held its breath.

A telegram arrived.

# PART 2

# AUTOBIOGRAPHY

There is a call to enjoy the little things in life, as upon reflection later, you may realise they were actually the big things. Autobiographical writers allow us the precious gift of a window into their lives, often mirroring these insights. In this section, the rugged texture of life in rural East Coast Aotearoa is depicted in *Saving Des* by Hughie Hughes, a tale of a rescue in limiting circumstances. Also set in this rural region is an unusual sighting in the Pakihiroa Valley, in *What We Saw That Night* by Alison McKay. Benita Kape takes us evocatively down memory lane to 1950s New Zealand summers at the bach in *Fifties Idyll*. Looking back at the start of a new life in Gisborne, Dan Witters recounts the journey of an adopted baby who travelled to the East Coast in a box in *View from a Fruit Box*. Well, his father used to jokingly say he'd been delivered in a fruit box ...

# SAVING DES

## HUGHIE HUGHES

Des was one of those guys we used to see around Ruatoria. Probably a veteran of WWII, who had quietly blended back into farming life, whether as a farmhand, a shepherd, a shearer, a fencer or a rouse-about. So glad to be back home from the horrors of war to a decent roof over his head, three square meals a day and the odd pint or two of ale. These stations were a real home-away-from-home for these men who, on the rare occasions when they went off farm, would catch up with their old mates and have to have a bit of a flare-up at the Ruatoria Pub.

My recollection of Pakihiroa history was about the turn of the century, when the station, comprising possibly around twelve thousand acres or thereabouts, was managed by a chap called Daddy Wickstead. The staff at that time would have been in excess of twenty men, plus families, with their own school and store. The station was at the base of 'the maunga', Mt Hikurangi, which lies across the Orinui River, twenty-five kilometres up the Tapuaeroa River from Ruatoria. In those days, the only access across the river for heavy goods was by bullock dray or horse and wagon. People wanting to cross may have had the use of a swing bridge. Over the years, with the loss of bush and the start of grazing, the riverbed continued to fill with debris from all the gullies above.

Len, a truck driver from Wards Transport, related to me that they used to be able to drive under the swing bridge with a truck loaded with wool with ease during the late 1940's. By the time I made my first journey up Mt Hikurangi in 1953, the bridge had disappeared altogether because of the rising riverbed. By the time of this incident I'm going to relate, a cage had replaced the old bridge, suspended by cable from towers on either bank. This cage was a metal structure with wooden panels, possibly the size of a small dining table, able to carry three to four persons at a time. There was a small box in the middle of the floor of this cage, in which sat a small two-stroke engine with a windlass mounted on the shaft.

For access from either side, the cage was retrievable with an endless rope. Once loaded, a free ride downhill to the middle of the river was achieved, the passenger starting the motor for the uphill pull by winding the rope a turn or so around the windlass.

So, the scene is now set.

One dark and stormy winter's night at about 7pm, I had a call from Colin Williams, the owner of the station. He alerted me (I was a Fireman and St. John Ambulance first aider), that Des, the shepherd at the station, had had a day off in Ruatoria. For his return he had hired a taxi to drive him back to the cable cage with his usual supply of beer. After sending Des off across the river in the cage, Snow, the taxi-driver, agonised about Des' safety getting across the river and called the station manager, Prince Rickard, enquiring whether Des had arrived home safely.

Prince checked and found Des was not in his hut. He then went to the station side of the cable and, aided by powerful torchlight, discovered the cage suspended in the middle of the flooded river above a small shingle mound. It appeared that Des' body had fallen out of the cage onto this small mound of shingle, about five metres below.

Now, on this very night, the Fire Brigade had their usual weekly practise meeting, which I could not attend due to visitors at home. After Colin's call, I notified the Brigade and we all sped to the scene in various vehicles. Having an electrical and hardware shop, I collected a large amount of nylon rope, adequate torches and batteries, and also a portable stretcher and first aid equipment which I used for my St. John Cadet group. We all met at the river, crossing in darkness, swollen river and pouring rain.

The key people with me were Colin Williams, the station owner, Ken McKinnon, Deputy Chief Fire Officer and a number of other firemen, including Arthur Hughes, my deputy in St. John and ex-scout leader, and George Newdick, a fireman and ex-scout. Evidently there was no movement from the body on the island, and we were not sure whether Des was alive or dead. The cage was pulled back to where we were. George, Arthur and I were selected to check out the situation and retrieve Des' presumed corpse. Then we were away.

The cage arrived above the shingle mound and I abseiled down to where Des' body lay. I found him still breathing but dead-to-the-world, and I heaved a great sigh of relief. However, it was impossible to lift his body back to the cage, so it was suggested that the crew on the riverbank haul us all back one by one, which was the most practical action to take. Colin Williams, in his wisdom though, said that was absolutely ridiculous, "they (us) would all drown!" and we heeded his advice.

So, imagine if you will, darkness, pouring rain, fast flowing river and here was Arthur and me assembling the collapsible stretcher in a very small area with Des still unconscious at our feet. We made strops on the four corners of said stretcher, with George supplying two lines fore and aft of the cage to tie onto the strops.

Having achieved this, we managed to suspend Des' body on the stretcher below the cage and just above the waterline. Arthur and I stayed behind, having little strength to get back up into the cage. Des was successfully winched ashore. George was sent back to pick up Arthur and me. A seat was made in the rope and Arthur, who hated heights, was the first person picked up and taken swiftly ashore. But the twist rope started to unwind and Arthur was spun round and round, very quickly becoming very disorientated. Thankfully, he arrived safely on the ground. For my return, a second rope was dropped to me from the other end of the cage to stop the rotation. Thus, I returned safely.

Before we had left Ruatoria we called the ambulance from Te Puia Springs, some sixty kilometres away, to ask them to attend. We were therefore surprised that the Ambulance had not yet arrived. The Chief Superintendent of the hospital, Dr George de Latour, was there, also wondering what had happened to the ambulance. What we found out later was that the ambulance driver had elected to go home to get more wet-weather gear, and got stuck in the soggy ground. While waiting for the ambulance to arrive, we actually had developed a thirst, and decided to dispose of Des' beer supply. However, we were put off when the doctor told us in no uncertain terms that Des was already suffering from hypothermia and needed better attention. We therefore complied!

Eventually, the ambulance did arrive, and Des was safely transported back to Te Puia hospital to dry out, in more ways than one. The rescuers, soggy wet and very cold, accompanied me back to my home, where we warmed up with the assistance of some whiskey which had been given to me (as a non-whiskey drinker) by suppliers.

A few days later, Des was sent home from hospital in good health after being well cared for by the staff.

The irony of that total situation was, within a couple of months, Des embarked on yet another liquid escapade, and was sadly killed outright, whilst driving his new boss's Land Rover.

# WHAT DID WE SEE?

ALISON MCKAY

*My husband and I spent the first three years of our married life teaching in a two-teacher school called Waiorongomai about eight miles out of Ruatoria in the beautiful Pakihiroa Valley. This valley is flanked by five mountains and is the gateway to Mt Hikurangi. What an amazing place to be part of, the people, the isolation, the stories told, the events that happened around us. Here is one.*

Driving home up the Pakihiroa Valley towards Mt Hikurangi, a very remote area, about midnight, 1957/58. I can still see the star-filled sky. No city lights here. One of those bright nights without a moon, when the silhouettes of the hills on either side of our valley were clear. It was probably about midnight and I was reflecting on the lovely dinner we'd been to with friends, thinking how isolated country people enjoy meeting and conversing. My thoughts were interrupted when my husband asked me if I'd noticed the bright star in the sky on my side of the car (the left). I replied that I'd noticed it too. Because it was so bright,

I'd first thought it was Venus but if so, I thought it should be on our right side. I'd been fortunate when as an eleven-year-old I'd gone to stay with friends who were amateur astronomers. I fancied I knew a bit about astronomy, as we had star-gazed every night with their range of telescopes.

We continued driving up the valley to where our house sat across the river from the smallest mountain in this chain, Taitai. We could see its outline as we drove nearer, the grassy slope on one side that led up to a sheer cliff face on the river side that faced our schoolhouse. The light seemed to be on the mountain. We pulled into our driveway and sat for a minute just watching and musing. Some locals must be on a shoot with a spotlight, we decided. We had been told that it was easy to ride a horse up the grass side. I got out of the car to open the gate and kept watching as I did so.

Suddenly the light moved down and then round the front, sheer, cliff side and disappeared out of view. I could feel the hairs on the back of my neck standing on end. I jumped back in the car and said, "Let's go further up the valley and see what is happening!" What we had seen was physically impossible. About a mile up the road we could see the full outline of Taitai again. We stopped the car and turned off our lights and engine. The light was there, suspended in the sky, motionless, soundless. The outline of Taitai was clear, the hills behind were clearly edged, the light just hung there in the sky while we stood speechless and spooked. Without a sound it suddenly moved off at a great trajectory, angling upward and diminishing in size, then it came angling back, still climbing, rapidly increasing size as it came nearer. Then it completed three more angles, zig-zagging and diminishing rapidly in a north-westerly direction, becoming a pinpoint and vanishing. Soundless, motionless, noiseless, the light could hover, go left, right and up and down as well as accelerate at amazing speed.

We stood there speechless, then we went over the facts, realising what we saw was unbelievable! During the next week we did some research. Only helicopters could hover. New Zealand had two helicopters in those days, one under repair in Wellington, one in the South Island.

We told a friend what we had seen and he told us we must have had too much to drink. No one believed us but this is as vividly clear to me today as it was seventy-three years ago.

# FIFTIES IDYLL

BENITA KAPE

*'and always at last everything follows,*
*the walk through the pines to the beach*
*the soft, suspended, hesitating air'*
Bill Manhire - from "Opoutere"

The government had not yet begun the building programme which would house the growing number of married personnel in Bulls nearer to the largest Air Force base in the country, Ohakea. For this reason, these men and their families sought accommodation in the many satellite towns within easy travelling distance, such as Feilding to the east and Foxton in the south. In beach communities like Foxton, accommodation was cheap and easy to come by, but the population at Foxton Beach swelled in summer and high rents over this period saw many of the servicemen and their families contending with eviction notices from their landlords. Often they opted to spend the full six weeks of the school holidays in tents in the plantation which stretched two sides of a natural basin. There were those who didn't mind this because they were closer to the sea, both literally and metaphorically.

It was 1953 and we secured a small bach at the back of a quarter acre section. Our bach was close to the river mouth and near a dairy. It was an ideal spot for a couple young and in love; our first home alone together after months of living in shared accommodation. To us it was sheer heaven and we had the added good luck of not having to do a summer 'move-out'.

Even in those days I enjoyed gardening and had a vegetable plot in the rich soil at the side of the bach. Giant macrocarpa trees on the southern boundary sheltered us from the wind and gave a climate of security and warmth. We had an outdoors loo at the back of the bach. In the kitchen we had a small wood burning stove no bigger than a camp oven, neither of which acted as drawbacks to our idyll.

Small as they were, both the sitting room and the bedroom were sun traps most of the day. The kitchen was roomy and accommodated a table. The table in the sitting room was repurposed from a caravan and built to the wall with caravan seats either side of it. Not exactly a dinner party set up. Across the narrow space was the caravan couch with squabs and a lid under which I stored books and trousseau treasures more likely for shelves and such like in the home we would one day work toward.

At first, I spent my days on the beach after my husband left for his day on camp as a signalman. The men travelled every day on the back of a canopied Ford truck, seated on wooden forms, and returned in the same manner each evening, a journey of almost an hour on those long straight roads in those days. Yet in today's fast-moving vehicles it takes half an hour or less. On Friday evenings the men arrived back a little early and the 'transporter' could be seen stationed outside the pub until closing time at six.

I readily found jobs, first in the flax factory engaged in making, among other things, wool packs. Flax grew readily in wetlands stretching for miles on the edge of town. Later I worked in a fish shop where consequently I got the sack because I wanted to take two weeks off to visit my in-laws when my serviceman husband took his Christmas furlough. But jobs were easy to come by so I happily moved on.

In the whitebait season, after work I would grab the whitebait net, and walk down to the creek. Within the hour available I would net a full billy of whitebait. Sometimes I'd hitch a ride back from the creek on 'the transport', as the boys called it. There was yet another drawback to living so far from camp. Every third week my husband had to do the graveyard (midnight to dawn-eight am) shift, and not having any means of transport home in the morning meant staying on camp for the full week. For a time, I didn't cope well with it and once begged my mother for her company while he was away. My dear mother obliged but I could see she was at a loss. Perhaps it was because I was from a large family and used to company constantly; perhaps it was that time of the month for me. Mother would never have pried, but seeing the alarm on her face I settled down and determined not to worry her again in such a manner. We enjoyed our week together and it became a mini holiday for my mother.

We lived the happy idyll for the next year until we moved to Feilding, which was much closer to Ohakea. Again, transport was provided, but before long we bought our own little Austin car. There being three shifts to each day, my husband arranged a day job in nearby Palmerston North, and the hours in that job now alternated with the shifts on camp.

At the end of a further three years, his twelve years of service in the Air Force completed, we followed through on his dream to return to his home town of Gisborne. Our second child had just been born and family life began in earnest.

I have been back to Foxton Beach a few times since then. The little bach is much closer to the river, which has since changed course. The dairy on the opposite corner to the macrocarpa trees has long gone. Anyone renting there now would need to get all their stores in town. The plantation I loved has gone and the whitebait creek is a polluted trickle.

# VIEW FROM A FRUIT BOX

DAN WITTERS

If anyone had told me the story I would have asked, "Why a fruit box?"

But not old Willie. He was a very practical man and he asked me, "What sort of fruit box?"

"Oranges. Queensland navel oranges."

"You sure?" he said, squinting at me.

"Does it matter?"

"Might do. Gotta have some relevance I suppose."

"No, it was just a box. A container. Could have been anything – a basket, a carton."

"Had to be big enough to put a baby in."

"Well, yes, obviously."

"And some blankets," he added. "They put blankets around you?"

"Must have I suppose. I was born in February, so it was the middle of summer. Would have been hot, but I guess they had to wrap me in something."

"Do you remember it?"

"No, how could I? I was only ten days old."

"I remember things from when I was that small," Willie replied.

"No you don't. They're false memories you constructed later in life. We're natural creators and imaginers and we flesh out our scant memories with things we make up."

"Don't you remember anything from that time?"

"Just a fern frond."

"Well, there you go then."

If you want to start with false memories, we could consider the clear one I have of my mother standing over my brother Michael's cot and playing with him as his head lolled and he dribbled. In the memory, she reaches down to him, which is difficult considering the high sides of the white wooden cot, and strokes his forehead. It's a crystal clear memory, but Michael died a year before I was born, so unless I've borrowed one of my mother's, and although theoretically the world might have that degree of plasticity, it's almost certainly a false memory that I've made up from things, like my mother sighing as she held a picture of Michael in his cot. Aunty Lelly used to take the family photos back then in the early fifties and then she used to paint over them to give the photos a sort of sanitised perfection.

I was adopted. That sounds akin to standing up in a room full of expectant faces and saying: "My name is Corwin Blake and I'm an alcoholic." Of the two I'd much rather be adopted. At least if you have a problem with that you can get drunk and forget it. Being an alcoholic is largely an unsolvable problem. Being adopted, if it's a problem at all, is only one of perspective.

I was born in Auckland, New Zealand and was quickly rerouted to the small beachside town of Gisborne, several hundred miles to the south. This sort of thing had been happening for quite a while.

We can inject some certainties into our investigation of my adoption by considering Section 7(4) of the Adoption Act 1955. This says the natural mother must consent to the adoption and can't do so until the baby is ten days old. A sort of cooling-off period of the type we have in hire purchase contracts these days, where the buyer has seven days to repent of his enthusiastic acquisition and take it back to the shop and admit that a mistake has been made. Prior to that it was a Dickensian free-for-all that allowed immediate post-birth snatching. So, at a minimum, ten days in the company of Mum. You'd think this would imply breast feeding, but in those days breastfeeding was viewed as a dangerous bonding between mother and child, so the mother was given cabbage leaves to ease the pain of her 'milk coming in' and the baby was given a glass bottle with a rubber teat and expected to extract cow's milk from it. Easy enough, it's a reflex action for the newborn. Who knows what nipples feel like if you've never sucked one?

Paperwork. There's always paperwork with these things. Humans love to record events. It's because we've always known what an unreliable tool memory is. I've been within inches of the paperwork, but the truth isn't there. The paperwork just records facts and those tell you almost nothing. You probably object to this and say that paperwork records what happened and so it must tell you something important. I'm not so sure. Corwin Blake, born 17 February, 1958, natural mother (redacted), adoptive parents Nelson and Millicent Blake, doesn't tell you much either. The answer isn't in the paperwork.

In my second birth I was delivered in the arms of a föhn wind. Its natural habitat is the pages of any old geography textbook, but it can appear in the real world where the natural flow of the world's winds drives one of them up a mountain slope forcing it to lose moisture and then to plunge down the far slope as a dry warming wind. When it takes this path, it is a sustaining and enhancing force. I arrived on a gentle wind.

An unnamed social worker brought me to my new home. Well, almost. I was presumably given to her in Auckland and she was charged with getting me to Gisborne. Maybe she didn't know about the disjunction that prevented train travel from being able to provide that; or maybe social workers have always been stupid. You can go from Auckland to Gisborne by train, but not directly. You have to go well south of Gisborne, to Napier, by a circuitous route and then trek north again. I think she knew this and was just too bloody lazy to do it. As far as I can tell, my parents' offer to drive to Auckland to collect me was rebuffed in favour of a Social Welfare Department directive to deliver the baby to the parents. Except that they couldn't, so a compromise was reached. Social Welfare would take me to the railhead at Taneatua where the Auckland train terminated, in fear of the Waioeka Mountains, and my parents would wend their way through the Waioeka Gorge in their Humber Super Snipe (with running boards) and collect me at the Taneatua Railway Station.


I'm lying in bed with my wife, Claire, my head resting on her bony shoulder, looking out to sea across Wainui Beach. Claire reaches over with her left hand and scratches my forehead in a manner that is vaguely affectionate, but more usually a precursor to a serious question.

"Why don't you go and look in the court records and find out who your parents are?"

"I know who my parents are. You met one of them."

"I mean your real parents."

"They are."

Claire moves her shoulder out from under my head, letting it drop onto a pillow. This is a sure sign she's annoyed.

"You know very well what I mean. Your birth parents."

"First or second birth?"

She moves away to the right, eliminating all physical contact between us from toe to temple. This is a sign that she is really annoyed with me.

"Stop it. You know exactly what I mean."

She's right, I do. We've had this conversation before. I accept that I have to answer her, but there must be some punishment for pulling away from me like that. After all, this is a marriage and no small slight can be allowed to go unpunished.

"Well, hard as it may be for you naturally-parented children to understand, I prefer to think of the people who brought me up and who were perfectly wonderful to me, as my parents. The others, the Grey Lynn schoolgirl and the Scottish sailor have to take a backseat in my affections, although even with all the imperfections that those imaginary DNA donors must have had, they may still equal your parents in the discharge of their parental duties."

This is a sally too far and Claire leaves the marital bed. I think that whenever the subject turns to parental origins I have a tendency to go too far.

I would like to think there was some memory involved in this next bit, but alas it is all imagined. Which is not to say that it's inaccurate. In fact, I think it won't be far from the literal truth. If I asked you to imagine what it was like at your birth you wouldn't be able to do it. After all, you can't even come to grips with a graphic image of your parents copulating at the time they created you. Can you? No. I don't have to approach that taboo area. I simply have to imagine my parents simulating the act of creation by driving through the Waioeka Gorge in the Snipe.

Actually, it wasn't even a train; it was a railcar. A diesel-powered couple of coaches that lacked any of the grandeur of a real train. From Auckland to Rotorua on a railcar and then decanted onto a freight train that had a smattering of passenger seats in the rear carriage. I know this much is true – I've researched it. We have to picture the nameless social worker lugging the fruit box with me in it from the railcar across to the other platform to catch the train to Taneatua. The metaphoric equivalent of a forceps delivery.

My parents arrived at Taneatua early. Of course, they did. My father was a chartered accountant so they may have been there days early for all I know. They spoke in truncated speech as they waited on the platform. The times of real engagement were past them. Michael's death had forged a rift. Their grieving was disparate; the father for what Michael might have been; the mother for the enormity of what he was. A dichotomy not easily resolved and those who cannot mourn in harmony must learn to live without it. What a couple they make on that empty platform. My father in a three-piece suit, restrained, but lacing the tension of the moment with thoughts of fly-fishing at Lake Waikaremoana and his other indulgences, while my mother, with her French heritage, uses exaggerated gestures and mannerisms as she paces the platform, a free spirit trapped in the straightjacket of hope.

Look at their movements. They pace and pirouette, impatient for my arrival; co-survivors of the Michael wars; borne down by the weight of expectation. She glances up and smiles at him. A restrained and nervous smile, but he sees buried in it the girl racing him up Motakio Hill, a child herself, with no inkling of motherhood in her. He wonders which of them will find more succour in the arriving child. It occurs to him that the expectations of both of them are extreme and unlikely to be fulfilled. He thinks of Michael's small coffin and wonders how his life can be so unbreakable among so much frailty.

There's no right time to tell a child he's adopted, but you can leave it too late. Or you can deliver it too early when the components of the concept won't mesh in the child's brain. Age five works well enough. My mother came into the bedroom and interrupted a game of balloon rugby I was playing. Poverty Bay (my team) was playing East Coast. Do I remember that? No, but those were the usual teams and in fact probably the only teams I knew, so they will do well enough.

"Corwin, I want to tell you something important. You were adopted. This means that you had another mummy besides me and another daddy. We went to Auckland and we met them and they just had too many children and they said to us, "We can't look after all these children, why don't you take our best one and let him live with you in your lovely place by the beach? I'm sure he'd be so happy there."

I know, it's clichéd, but don't judge her harshly. What would you say to a five-year-old in those circumstances? I pretty much bought it, although as far as I recall, when the game resumed after that speech it was the only occasion that East Coast managed to beat my team at balloon rugby.

The curse is that I became a lawyer and you can imagine what a lawyer does in imaginary conversation with his dead mother, cross examining her over that little piece of history. You can pick the flaws in the narrative without much difficulty. You wouldn't give away the best one and at ten days you wouldn't have much idea about how he was performing anyway. The whole thing lacks credibility and so the adopted child is obliged to construct a counter-narrative. Mine goes like this: sixteen-year-old girl from Grey Lynn has disastrous and not entirely consensual (important component that one) sexual encounter with Scottish seaman in … well, actually the exact location is singularly unimportant apart from say, Auckland. This is a much better story, because adoption becomes an obvious necessity.

There's always something slightly suspicious about those poor, loving, Disney parents with exactly one too many children. A Grey Lynn school girl can have all the potential you want to invest in her. She hasn't failed yet, the ill-advised coitus notwithstanding, and she may well go on to be magnificent despite her unrequited yearning to be reunited with her first born. The Scottish seaman can be as clever as you like. As a second son falling victim to the cull of primogeniture, who knows what drove him to sea? He may well have been a romantic figure, a rover, a charmer, a lover of balloon rugby. I may have inherited some of these traits from him.

The train pulls into the station and my mother can't help herself. The birth is imminent and she is naturally drawn to the father by an impulse too strong to ignore. She takes his hand and involuntarily steps back from the power of the approaching train. He stands firm. The social worker, a dumpy woman in her early fifties, past child-bearing age, departs the train, turning the fruit box sideways to allow her to exit the narrow door. My mother slips her silken hand from my father's grip and races towards the quarry. There is no doubt conversation. Only this is relevant.

"I'm so sorry about the box. He was in a bassinet when we left Auckland, but I jammed it in the door when we were getting on the train and it ripped apart. I was holding the baby and an old Māori man sitting opposite me asked me how far I was going. When I told him Taneatua, he said, 'You can't hold a baby all that way, girl, let me make a bed for you in this crate.' And he tipped all the oranges from the box into a sack he had, and we put the blankets into the orange box and put baby 136 in it. He's been so comfortable he's slept most of the way."

My mother carries the fruit box. My father feels instinctively that he should be carrying it and in fact he thinks the baby should probably be removed from the contraption, but his views are irrelevant. I am in the arms of a woman who had been little able to cuddle her first child and had to engage with him from the confines of a high-sided cot. Me in the fruit box held close to her face is a new intimacy. And she screens me for defects. She doesn't have to explain this impulse to my father in terms he could understand.

She reaches the Snipe and puts one foot up on the running board. My father, ever the gentleman, opens the front passenger's door for her and she stares at him with blank incomprehension. "You idiot, I will sit in the back seat with our new son. Did you seriously think I would sit in the front with you and leave the baby in a fruit box in the back seat?"

"It's okay, Mum, the view from a fruit box is fine."

And so we drove through the Waioeka Gorge and home to Gisborne, a gentle föhn wind at our back. In the course of our passage through the birth canal that the narrow gorge must represent, I had the only true memory contained in this story. I clearly recall the unfurled fern fronds hanging over the edge of the road. Are they important? I don't know. The more you stand back from your life and paraphrase it, the more you see metaphor. A railway line that ends. A flawed midwife that takes you from a mother and hands you to new parents.

I chased Claire into the bathroom and snatched her arm. "I'm sorry. I don't mean to be defensive about it. I could have known everything about my mother. The adoption was put thorough in Gisborne. I'm an Officer of the court. I have an unfettered right to search Court documents. I've been into the Court records section several times. It's alphabetical. Adoptions are the first set of files. I've been right up to mine and touched it. All I had to do was take it off the shelf and open it. But I knew that would have been a betrayal. My real mother was the wonderful woman who brought me up and died when I was twelve. She's proved to be more than a handful. I don't need any other mothers. I have no animus against the Grey Lynn girl. I bless her for bringing me into this place and I hope she's okay. But she's not my mum."

Claire looked at me closely and then stroked my cheek with the back of her hand. She's not an overly demonstrative woman but we both know that that gesture means she loves me and more importantly she approves of me.

Was it easy being adopted? Pretty much. I arrived amidst two families that between them contained thirty-nine first cousins in the small town of Gisborne and they took me to their collective breast. There were the occasional moments of discord. My cousin

Hugh once said to me during an argument that at least he knew where he came from. It hurt at the time, but those of us who travel early in fruit boxes learn certain survival skills. I noticed that his father, my uncle Deacon, was as bald as a bandicoot and the photos in the den at their house suggested that his grandfather had been the same. You'll find that adopted children are fairly *au fait* with matters of genetic inheritance and so I was able to alert him to the fact that alopecia would strip him of his head hair early in life. I waited to deliver this piece of bad news until it would have maximum impact, 1973, when I was the guitarist in a rock band and had long, flowing locks virtually stretching to my coccyx and Hugh had long, but thinning hair. The length of a young man's hair in the early seventies assumed an importance not seen since the days of Samson.

And I made it worse. I gave his nemesis a name – alopecia. And I made it worse still with a dreadful pun to etch it into his memory. I told him his impending condition sounded like a greeting to a Polish prostitute. I knew that corny as it was, he'd never budge that one from his mind. So, Hughie, you can revel in knowing where you came from, but the corollary of that is I can show you where you're going. And that's one of the adopted child's primary joys. The blank slate. Your parents may die of cardiac problems or testicular cancer, but it has no relevance for you. You are an unknown commodity, free from antecedents, born into the world pristine, trailing clouds of glory, free from family, caste and class, unless you choose to adopt one.

I inherited my parent's home on the beach, and I keep the fruit box in the garage. My father used to tease me about it and ask me even in my teenage years whether I thought I could still fit into it. He kept it on a high shelf above the cupboard where he kept spare parts for machinery like the lawn mower. You couldn't say my conveyance took pride of place. I left the fruit box to gather dust in the garage.


Willie and I sat there on the front lawn looking out to sea. Claire had gone for a walk on the beach and left me in charge of the newest of our three children, Benjamin, who was only a couple of months old. He was asleep in the shade of his pram. And then the old boy had a great idea.

"Corwin, why don't you put Benjamin in the fruit box to see how it looks?"

I was going to tell him not to be so stupid and then I thought, "Why not?" I went to the garage and got it down off the cupboard, gave it a bit of a dust-off with a towel and brought it back to the front lawn. I set it down between me and Willie and lifted Ben with all his swaddling clothes and blankets and popped him in the fruit box. He woke up and appeared to stare out to sea, thrusting his glance over the rim of the fruit box, newest scion of a family line that now stretched back almost forty years, trapped in the certainty of his heredity.

# PART 3

# THAT YEAR CALLED 2020

The less said about 2020, the better. With a few well chosen words Susan Partington puts you into the empty streets and diaries of lockdown in *How to Survive 2020*. Rodney Baker gives us a virtual window into this new world, when even grieving and tangihanga must take place via digital means, in his touching poem, *My Sister*. In her *Letters from Lockdown* Gillian Moon's poems give us a series of unique and rich New Zealand images. With a deceptively simple *Haiku*, Karen Morris-Denby conveys a melancholic snapshot of a park. Ruth E. Helmling's poem, *Lockdown*, speaks to an emotion that usually helps us get through problems, but during this modern plague is hard to cling to. *In the hole*, by Claire Price, paints a slice of this new life, with its rules and anxieties.

# HOW TO SURVIVE 2020

SUSAN PARTINGTON

You step outside on the first morning of lockdown and the silence stuns you. No steady rumble of cars and trucks. You wonder if this is how the world will end, not with a bang but with a peaceful stillness. You've always jumped to the worst conclusions, 'assume apocalypse' is your motto.

It's unsettling to fear a tiny, invisible enemy, like being trapped in a science fiction movie, set on your own sofa. You feel like a child home sick from school, watching T.V. and eating junk food while the adults make all the decisions for you. You lay on the floor and listen to entire albums, like you did when you were a teenager and life was eternal. When did music become background noise, just the soundtrack to your busy life? Now a piano solo can make you cry.

You see photos of empty New York streets and remember that hot summer when you pressed up to strangers on dance floors and subway cars. Are some of those bodies being buried in mass graves on Hart Island? Rows of plain pine boxes, gravediggers in hazmat suits. You remember the hustle of those city streets and mourn the vitality of the city finally put to sleep.

Years collapse, minutes stretch endlessly, you cannot trust time.

You cross out everything in your diary. You turn each page cancelling jobs, parties, meetings, until you finally shut and shelve the book and wonder how you will fill your days. Your to-do list becomes your ta-da list. Ta-da! A homemade loaf of bread. Ta-da! A completed jigsaw puzzle. Ta-da! Waves of anxiety surfed without drowning. In these moments of crushing sadness, you wonder why you chose to have kids. What does their future hold? You clutch at their warm bodies in bed while they clutch their stuffed toys. A soft embrace to muffle the fear. You want to hide inside their innocence.

You miss your friends, seeing people you know, but what you really miss is being seen. *Look at me!* you shout from the depths of your soul. Does an extrovert even exist in isolation? Across the still dark night, you hear a Ruru call his own name and you wait for the answer.

# MY SISTER

RODNEY BAKER

Covid-19 Tangihanga
You have to do it right.
When the rawness of life – stares you in the face
And the pandemic is at your door step
When someone you love – has had their time
of grace upon this earth.
And it is eternal sleep for them.
Manakotutahi – at Mangatuna
God bless her soul to keep
The eulogy and whakapapa spoken
We hear the names of whanau given
By Wayne James – and he recalls
The Urupā where the family are resting
In yonder graves, over there.
An historical footprint of time past –
that my Sister now shares.
A modern facetime moment –
When live-stream makes us aware

With picture – script – conversations –
In actual time to appear – on phone
Screens with speakers and movement –
To talk to the family – that have no
Chance to come. Here.

On another continent – it is all crystal clear.
We can mourn – grieve – be joyous –
Until the day when we all stand here.

# LETTERS FROM LOCKDOWN

GILLIAN MOON

Foreword:

During 2020 lockdown, as many of us would have, I put in place several practices to ease myself into this new way of living. I viewed this as an opportunity to recharge, reset, reboot. Meditation and writing were at the forefront of my list. I write this on day thirty-two; I have meditated and written daily, formed a habit which is now as automatic as my daily walks or bike rides. Of course, there have been challenges and "what's the point?" days, and some days I have written ramblings of nonsense, even questionable to myself.

However, I have also learned not to berate myself, nor judge my written work. I joined online courses in poetry, writing and meditation and as each one came to an end I found myself carrying on with the practices that had been put in place. This has become my measure of my success.

I offer here a selection of letters and poetic verse all written during lockdown 2020.

Namaste.

## Letter to Last Year's Self

Dear 2019 Self,
How are you doing back there?
It's amazing for me to have time,
not only to sit
but to sit and write!

There is of course a back-story,
yet more about that later.
Last year was an upheaval of mammoth portions huh?
Dying, Death, Loss and Grief
all with capitals
hit us like a ton of
torpedoed rocks

No matter how we dodged
we still got hit
I feel kinda sad
you are still back there
in struggle street

Yet, would like you to know
that resilience you are
showing and building on
right now

will keep you balanced
and steadfast in the future
to come

There is lightness coming
there are still tears
there is still sadness
it's ... somehow just different
now

Anniversaries have come
and gone
healing rituals
and letting go
new babies
welcomed to the fold
much to look forward to

and much to fear
as I said earlier
that resilience you are building
it has become our middle name
add kindness,
add compassion

ingredients for 2020
life
No one saw it coming
and I will not elaborate
here
just take my advice
keep meditating,

keep stretching body, mind and
soul
keep writing and knowing
all you do is for the
Higher Good.

Bring openness
bring patience
bring hope

Keep working through your grief
it has got us where we need to be
handling 2020
with a new perspective

Namaste dear Self
Be Well
Go Well

Love and light
from your 2020 Self.


## The Isle of Gillian Moon

I could give you directions
yet I doubt you would be able to
cross that border.

I will wave, nod and smile.
You may not see me behind
my mask

and sunglasses
so you probably wouldn't know if
I was smiling
at all.

Daily walks for sanity
Friend or foe?
hooded, balaclava clad
trouble
or
simply for protection.

Distance is called for
Stay in your 2-metre bubble
Do not leave your bubble
Do not share your bubble
Do not, under any circumstances
burst your bubble!

My bubble is shared
with two teenagers
I am armed with
good food, humour
and wine
definitely wine.

I cheers my friends
on video calls
adorning myself
with funny face
filters.

Poised in a home
piled with packed
boxes
ready and
primed
for our new abode.

Island hopping is prohibited at this time!


## Pandemic Gratitude

A Toast to the Necessary Workers

Cheers mate
Salute
Chin chin
Prost
Slainte
Kanpai
Bottoms up
Chur bro
Here's to you
with thanks
with blessings.


## My Name is Hope

There's a rainbow hiding
in this shit sandwich situation

Where there is darkness
I see light

Where there is conspiracy
I seek my own truth

I see
I smell
I hear
I taste and
touch
Hope

In the beginning it was a flicker of light,
I saw,
I nurtured,
tended and
cared for
through meditation,
yoga,
writing

I gave that flicker
my energy
and time
… fear retreated
… anxiety melted

I am grateful for
rest time
recharge time
reset and

reboot

My name is Hope
I live in abundance
with my daughters
Resilience
Acceptance
Peace and
Wisdom

Collectively we got this.


## Taking Moments

Making space
clearing clutter
inside
brain whizzing
with neurons
like crazy ants
colliding like
constellations
in an exploding
night sky

Taking time
to slow it
all down
breaking it down
to bite size
baby steps of

thought
word,
deed

There is much to do
yet nothing at all

I am watching the shadow of hand
scroll across paper

I hear gentle scratch of pen
exploring page

I feel breath and body
relax

I smell fresh, fragrant
morning air

I taste the lingering
remains of sleep

As my home stirs and
awakens

I am grateful for
this new day.

Blessed be.

**Solo**

In my mind's eye
I have travelled
coast to coast
East to West

Returning home
to windswept iron-rich
black beach
dense native New Zealand bush
dripping in dew drops
glow worm jewels
at night
the solo lament
of Ruru keeping its
nightly vigil
Wild west coast
waters
hurling forth its perils
winds that catch your breath
and fling your voice away
into the literary ether
fresh waterfalls
and opal pools

I am home
solo and
at peace
not a fellow
human being
in sight.

I yearn my childhood
place
locked in my
heart.

Locked in my house,
in the East
locked under house arrest
feeling trapped now
can't breath
can't move
can't scream
neighbours
will freak
walking on eggshells
don't cough or sneeze
seasonal allergic rhinitis
no swimming allowed
so I pour salt waterfalls up
my nose and
pretend it's doing the trick
when clearly
it is not.


## Kitchen Slop

Like a parasite
under my skin
constantly niggling
squirming

irritating
is the status
of my lock-down kitchen
slop

Add two teenagers,
who like to bake,
who eat constantly throughout
the day,
and we are not talking a quick sandwich,
we're talking overflowing spaghetti toasties,
pastas, hash browns, falafels, spinach, and
absolute frigging
mountains of grated carrot and cheese.

Don't get me onto cereal bowls,
for those who know,
that crusty shit
sets like cement

Smoothies are also flavour of the day
stained benches of berry fruit
dripping down cupboards
so they look like
artwork

If it's not on the bench
you guessed it
it's made its way to the floor

A million glasses and cups
WTF! can't they just use one!

Not a single piece of cutlery
left in the drawer.

No, we do not have a dishwasher per se
we actually have three,
One, with encouragement
does amazing work
the other,
eventually responds well to yelling
to complete a half-assed job
and the main one
which would be me,
has decided in total frustration
to go on strike
indefinitely!


## Hugs Withheld

Alert Level 4

'do not hug, cuddle, kiss hello or goodbye,
do not hongi
keep 2 metres apart at all times'

five long
arduous
weeks

oxytocin, dopamine and
serotonin
deprived

not a whisper of a hug
in the wings

no cuddles
with grand-baby
newborn
in
lockdown

am feeling deprived
skin hunger
touch hunger
of love

a slow
withering
form
of torture

not abstinence
as it is not
my choice.


**Thoughts on holding Ava Audrey-Rae
for the first time today**

Broke my bubble
for a stolen moment
of love so pure...

a gift received
delicate, vulnerable life
Newborn bliss
a life
pulsating in my arms
staring through eyes
of knowing
hearing my voice
feeling my love
my unconditional
Grandmotherly love.


**Letter to Future Self**


Dear 2021,


Are we there yet?
And by that I mean
are we living our best life?


I hope the lock-down
is now a distant memory
and we as a race
have continued to look
after our beautiful Mother Earth.


Our book/s will surely be published,
launched and meeting with
great success.


Life will be sunny

carefree,
dancing and
free

I can't wait to see
what amazing job
I have
utilizing my
skills in
social work
in a deep and meaningful way.

Feeling fulfilled
with perhaps a special friend
sharing and nurturing
Is he that beautiful, hippy kinda of guy
I sometimes see on my daily out of lock-down
nature walks?
I sense connection!
Excited much!

Daughters will be shining
Each in their own way
Granddaughters will be thriving
and keeping you on your toes.

Have you travelled by rail
to the South Island yet
I can't wait to experience that.

I so look forward to this fantastical
space that you are

reclaiming,
loving and
living
your best Self.


See you when I get there


Love and light
from your 2020 locked-down
dreaming
Self.

# HAIKU

KAREN MORRIS-DENBY

Anzac Park stands still
Waiting for the kids to play
Lockdown bans all fun

# LOCKDOWN

RUTH E. HELMLING

seeping creeping
soul sucking
traitor, you,
take in those tentacles of yours
ensnaring
my dreams
my thoughts
my very soul
dissipate that subjunctive glow
haloing your presence
and my future
delete those promised lands
dilute those vivid colours
go, just go!
go back into your hole
shut the door
leave me, leave me
alone but whole

as I was before
without missing
without thinking
without dreaming
without you,
hope

# IN THE HOLE

CLAIRE PRICE

Welcome to our camped-in space,
The race
To find sanity and comfort
With a limited pool of others.

The rooms we inhabit
With our bodies,
The places we frequent
In our minds,
Together
We are stitched,
Like seams in a garment,
Made to work in unison, for now,
Yet able to be unpicked and
Repurposed, if need be,
Once things change.

We each filter

In and Out
Of the exits from home,
Solitary
Or in pairs,
We join the ranks of others
In the street,
On the beach,
Along the river,
Walking, cycling, jogging,
Talking to neighbours,
From our anti-social distance,
Our thinly-veiled movements towards
Connection.

One of us per household
Makes the journey
For supplies,
Masks and gloves adorned,
Our faces carefully avoiding too much
Contact
With others,
While we stand in line outside the shop,
Feeling awkward
In avoiding physical intimacy,
So unused to not hugging
Friends and family
We see there.

Once inside the shop, we maintain
Our walls,
Ever vigilant
Of the rules,

Mindful of not stockpiling,
Yet conscious of our human instinct
To survive and protect
Our families.
Lining up to pay,
Keeping our distances from each other,
Smiling weakly at the cashier
Behind the large Perspex shield,
Stepping back to avoid
Accidentally touching each other
Over the bread.

Our guards intensify over time
As we adjust to this new mentality,
Aware of the shoulds and
Shouldn'ts,
We become the new police,
Condemning those who break the
Rules,
Keen that our collective sacrifices not be
In vain.
Or so we say.

We watch or read the news,
Some obsessively,
Until our anxiety moves into
Overwhelm,
When we decide that
Watching cute or funny videos
And exercising
Will keep us saner.

We worry about our jobs,
Our businesses,
How we'll continue to
Pay the bills,
How safe we'll be,
What the new normal will be
When all this is over.

Our children's educations
Change
Overnight -
Virtual schooling
The only option,
Motivation and
Self-discipline
The biggest lessons
For our kids now.

Some of us focus on the
Positives -
More quality time with family,
Less pollution,
Less consumerism,
Time to learn a new skill,
Resting, recuperating,
Clarity about what's
Important
Now.

We all went
Into the hole
On 25 March

2020.

How we emerge
From it
Might depend on
What shapes us
In there,
And what makes the
Cut,
To bring out with us.

# PART 4

# GRAPHIC STORY

Words can create a mental image in the mind of the reader. They paint a picture in the mind, and this picture is sometimes even more vivid than what the writer conceived. In the selections of this anthology so far, the writers have endeavoured to reach not only all of your senses, but your emotions as well. But there is another type of writing, the type that uses graphic images as its main tool. In the following pages we are treated to a story not of words, but pictures, a graphic novel, if only a day long. *Another Day*, by Ruth E. Helmling, follows the sun, where the sun shines first.

# Another Day

RUTH E. HELMLING

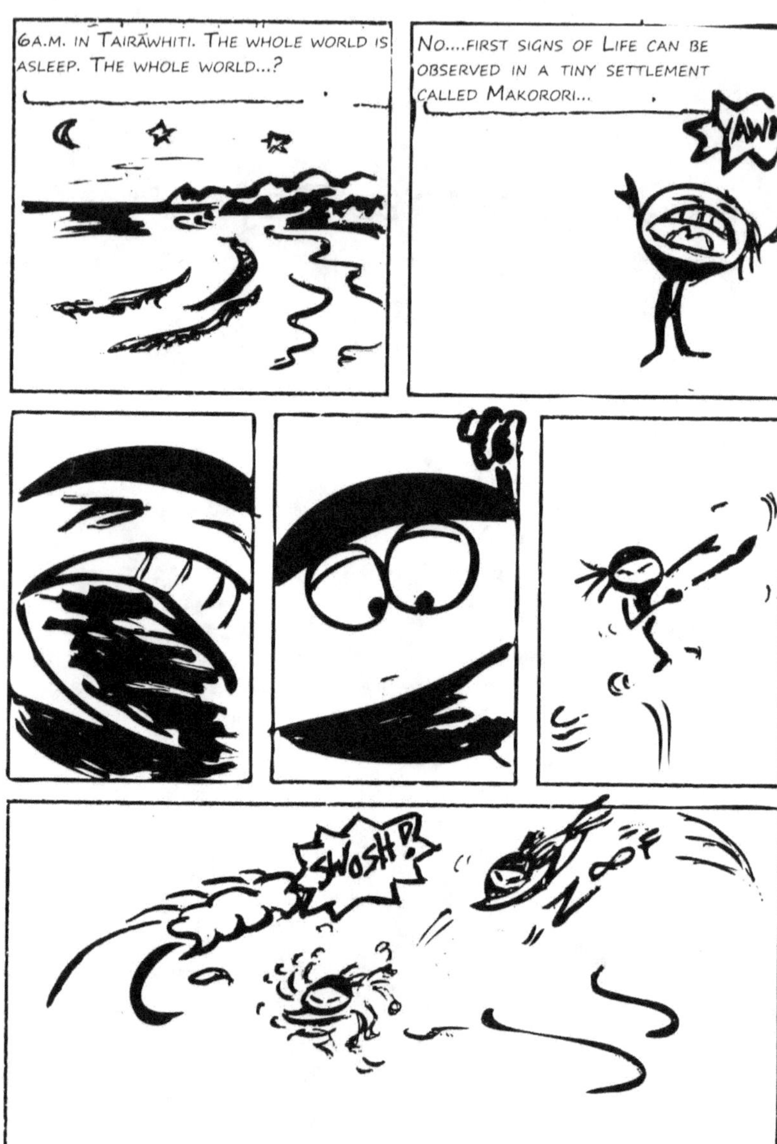
6A.M. IN TAIRĀWHITI. THE WHOLE WORLD IS ASLEEP. THE WHOLE WORLD...?
NO....FIRST SIGNS OF LIFE CAN BE OBSERVED IN A TINY SETTLEMENT CALLED MAKORORI...
YAWN
SWOSH!

MEANHWILE ON THE OTHER SIDE OF THE HORIZON....
ZZZZ
TOC TOCK
WAKE UP SUN! RISE & SHINE
tomorrow... you said.... that's TODAY

HMMF
VUAAAWGHH!
TRRNGM

AND SO THE SURFERS FROM MAKORORI
BEACH STARTED YET ANOTHER DAY FOR
THE UNIVERSE.
THE END

# PART 5

# KAITUHI RANGATAHI

Neil Gaiman said, "a book is a dream you can hold in your hands." In the following stories and poems by young people in this book we aim to encourage the desire to grow and learn as writers. In *Pride*, Hannah Reulens describes the immortal personification of a deadly sin who is contemplating his retirement. Lyra Caughley introduces us to a ghost who mourns her place in a lost world, in her story *Paint Eternity*. The poem titled *Home*, by Josiah Goddard, shows us that home is more than a place. Henarata Kohere Pishief retells the story of a Greek nymph in her poem *Eurydice*. With the poem *Dawn*, Jashan Kaur takes us to the most transient moment of a new day. The characters in Jacqueline Te Kani-Nankivell's ghost story, *The Missing Science Partner*, come to terms with grief and guilt while making a scientific breakthrough. Moana Hoogland introduces the source of her own personality, with images of her interests, activities, and her place, in her poem, *I am from*. And Roman Seaton weaves a dark tale about a desperate lawyer trying to complete a deal in *The Wrongs of the Marshlander*.

# PRIDE

## HANNAH RUELENS

*Maybe I should consider passing on the title. I cannot afford to keep making mistakes like this.* Derrick closed his eyes and shook his head, as if to erase the very thought of that failure from his mind. *It's not just the recent incident either. I've made so many mistakes over the centuries. If I do decide to pass on my powers ...* Derrick paused for a moment, looking pained, before continuing his train of thought. *Then I need to make sure that it is someone who won't make the same mistakes I did. That means I need to go out there and find them personally. If I cannot find anyone more suited to the role, I could always stay Pride for a bit longer.* He nodded decisively before standing up and walking out of the house.

Five hours later, he sank down on a bench, exhausted. Who knew finding someone filled with pride would be so hard? He felt a whole new respect for the old Pride, who had searched for months before finding him as a replacement. Then again, maybe it's not that hard. He had, after all, found a lot of people with pride – the pianist at his favourite coffee shop, the skater in the park and even the local hairdresser – just none that he would want as his replacement. They all had pride in being good at what they did and there was nothing wrong with that. But all of them also had a selfish edge to that pride. A sense of feeling superior because of that skill and that was something he couldn't accept for the position of Pride. If he did, that selfishness would only grow with the extra power the job provided. If there was anything his past mistakes had taught him, it was that a feeling of superiority was bound to cause problems. His powers could wreak a lot of havoc in the wrong hands. He refused to hand that much power to someone undeserving. Not again.

The problem, he decided, was that it was extremely hard to find someone without that sense of superiority. It was almost a human trait. Whether it was connected to their looks or their skills, they all held it, even if only a small spark. So how on Earth was he supposed to ... Derrick stopped his inner monologue and looked up, as he had registered a presence in front of him. A young woman, probably in her twenties, was standing before him, shyly wringing her hands.

"Is it okay if I sit here?" she asked.

For a few seconds, Derrick debated the issue. Sure, it would be rude to decline, especially as it was clear that he wasn't waiting for anyone, but he also didn't want to deal with the inevitable questions that would follow if he allowed her to sit next to him. Then again, he thought, sizing up her shy demeanour, that probably wouldn't be a problem with her. So, he nodded in answer and watched her sit down. She stayed silent and he returned to considering his issue, but quickly realized he couldn't focus now that someone was sitting next to him. He gave in and asked for her name.

"Martha," she answered, a whisper almost, "and you?"

"Derrick."

An awkward silence followed. Derrick had never been good with social conventions, as they changed rather fast from his perspective. He simply nodded and tried once more to get back to trying to find a solution for his problem. A soft voice, however, disrupted that process.

"What's bothering you?"

A simple question, and yet he had no idea how to answer it. How could he explain his problems in terms she would understand? She was watching him expectantly and so he tried, improvising as he went along.

"Well," he started, "I have a very specialised job, with rigid requirements. I've recently realized that I might not be such a good fit for it anymore, but cannot find anyone else that fills the requirements either."

He realised he had started waving his hands and raising his voice, so quickly lowered his voice again.

"It's just bothering me a bit, that's all."

He looked back to where she sat listening, head cocked to one side.

"Why do you think you're not suited for it anymore?" she asked.

This time, Derrick could not suppress a flinch. He mumbled an "I'd rather not talk about it," but in his mind, he was already reliving that night.

It should have been simple, but it was almost his downfall. Lessons drilled into his brain so long ago, forgotten until far too late. Always be the one to pick the meeting place. Don't tell anyone all your weaknesses. Have a back-up plan. He had been so lucky to find a different way, something he hadn't known about and therefore couldn't tell others. Why had he wanted to share all that information anyway? Maybe he had just wanted to talk about himself for once, let everything out. He wanted to do that now as well, but refrained. After what occurred last time, he wouldn't let it happen again.

As his thoughts turned back to his companion, he realised that she had not moved. He had been zoning out a lot recently. Maybe he was getting old. Of course, he'd also had a lot on his mind lately.

"So," she said, "a colossal screw-up that endangered everything you love and stand for? Yeah, me too. But I'm not sure that I could fix it by simply resigning like you want to. So now, here I am, on a park bench with a stranger, trying to figure out what to do with the rest of my life. Wow, that's not what I thought my Friday would look like."

Derrick smiled despite himself and soon a couple of hours had passed. Once she got out of her shell, Martha was actually a pretty good conversationalist.

"Hey, I should get going," Martha said, when she finally noticed how dark it had become. "I don't know where I'm going yet, but I should at least start figuring that out."

Derrick had the immediate impulse to ask her to come home with him, but refrained. This was something she had to discover on her own, just like he had to decide what to do after the latest disaster. There he was, thinking about it again. He let out a sigh. Martha must have heard his sigh, because she wryly smiled at him.

"Well, at least you didn't think about it for a bit, right?" she observed.

Derrick realised that he hadn't once thought about his problem in all those hours of conversation.

"Yeah, yeah I didn't. Thanks for that."

He smiled at her and was surprised by the soft feeling of pride he could feel in Martha. He observed she experienced a sense of a job well done, but without the feeling good about yourself that usually came with it. How peculiar. Maybe it had something to do with her screw-up, which he still knew nothing about. He had, after all, tried just as hard to distract her from her problems as she had to distract him from his. Whatever the cause, she was exactly what he was looking for.

On the other hand, he couldn't ask her right now. He realised she needed to overcome her mistake before being able to move on. Like he had, just now, when he saw that he had finally found a way to make sure his mistakes would not keep repeating themselves. Maybe he could offer her his card, tell her to give him a call when she had forgiven herself, that he would have a job waiting for her? So, he did.

Three months later, Derrick received a call.

# PAINT ETERNITY

LYRA CAUGHLEY

Someday, the world will end.

And countless years later, a ghost will scramble down an over-grown hillside. The ghost will be formless, shapeless, a beast with no soul or memory. Yet it will be drawn to this place, for reasons it can't quite comprehend.

It will come to a ruin ensnared in a crippled iron fence. Suddenly, a rush of sensations: birdsong, churning water, barbed wire silhouetted against a grey sky. The smell of leaf litter, dampness and decay, a heaviness in the air and a feeling of being watched. Trees will sigh in the wind, as if the forest is exhaling.

The ghost will survey the ruin – the rust and peeling paint and rain slick concrete. A cluster of skeletal buildings will be huddled together like animals seeking warmth. One will be a pump house, its mechanical innards laid bare, belching oil onto the grass. Another will be a changing room with cracked windows and rotting benches.

Driven by urgency and a sudden aching loneliness, the ghost will melt through the fence and discover a swimming pool. Memories will flood back.

*Right now, her name is Anna.*

*She's sitting with her toes dangling above the pool, listening to the splashes of divers and the lazy thrum of cicadas. Heat shimmers above scorching concrete. The smell of pollen and freshly mown grass is thick in every breath. A seagull glides above her, its wings outstretched, squawking and playing with the lazy summer wind.*

*Anna loves to paint, and she's certain that one day she'll manage to capture the beauty here. She'll show everyone the ripples of light on the dark underbelly of the pumphouse, the sprawling meadow and the forested hills arching away to meet the sky.*

*"Anna!" Her brother Jack comes running towards her, shattering her daydreams. "We're leaving now. Grandma says –"*

*Anna sticks out her tongue and plunges into the pool. Coolness and silence embrace her. Jack's distorted face glares at her through a broken film of water. Her laughter explodes in a stream of bubbles as she rockets towards the far wall, heart pounding with joy.*

The ghost, no longer nameless, will regard the pool with a quiet sorrow. The walls will be cracked and overgrown with moss, scored with ancient graffiti. At the bottom, a faded milk bottle will rattle to and fro in the wind. Ghostly tears will well up, and another memory will surface.

*She vaults the stone wall and runs up the bank, dripping wet and panting, her eyes still stinging with chlorine.*

*"Grandma, you said you were gonna swim."*

*"I'm too old, dear."*

*Anna fumes. "Come* on, *it'll be more fun if you're there. Look, Jack's swimming too now."*

*Grandma flashes her a warning look. "Anna –"*

*"Fine." Anna laughs. "Whatever."*

*She plops down on her back, her hands tucked under her head. Dry grass tickles her arms. Beyond the weeping willow and the gnarled kanuka trees are snatches of bright sky. She used to pretend the clouds were islands afloat in an ocean of blue, and on a day like today, she could almost believe it.*

*Today feels special, after all. Almost magical.*

Anna will weep.

Ghostly tears will drip from her cheeks and slither down the pool walls. She'll shudder and bury her face in her hands, stunned at the knowledge of everything she's lost.

Then she'll raise her head and scrutinize the ruin again, as if she's truly seeing it for the first time. She'll notice the puddles of green algae, the spider web under the awning, the birds darting through the canopy. Even amidst the stench of rust and oxidising metal, saplings will wrestle for the brightest shafts of sunlight. A brutal feeling of peace will overwhelm Anna, and she will begin to fade. She'll wipe away her tears because ... it's all so *alive.*

The clouds will fray to reveal an indigo ribbon of sky. Evening light will wash over the land. By the time the first stars have appeared, Anna will be gone.

# HOME

JOSIAH GODDARD

I was born somewhere
Now I do not live there

When I was young
I came from afar
From where I was born
To here where we are

From the land of the free
To the long white cloud
Now the home where I live
Will soon vanish from sight
And our family again
Shall soon take flight

To a new place
A new house
To new memories

To a new yard
A new bed
A new set of keys

And I think to myself
Where is home?
Well let me tell you
Something true
Home is with my family
Home is with you.

# EURYDICE

HENARATA KOHERE PISHIEF

Light, finally
I'm almost there, almost home
Your voice echoes
Your songs fill the silent void between us
You sing of our lives
What has been and what could happen
And we're so close
So close to the promised forever

And then you turn
Going against the guidance given to you by the gods
I feel myself slipping back
Back into the abyss
Your song of forever, your song of our future
Stops dead as you see me drift
Gone for the second time in our lives

And this can't be happening

After all you went through
Your pained efforts to revive me
Thrown away in an instant
You were always so determined
This can't be real
You convinced the king and queen of the dead to let me live
Something no mortal had done
Yet you still let me fade, fade back into hell

For days I crawl
Fighting the intangible chains that keep me here
And all that plays in my mind is you
How you turned around before I was safe
How you can live on without me
If I could get to you
If only I could get to you
Then everything would be okay

My days and nights are spent at the gates of hell
My hands bloody and calloused
I can't get to you
Clawing at the walls, the floors, the ceiling
I can't get to you
What did I do to deserve this eternal punishment
I can't get to you

The only thing that separates me from all the wandering souls
Is my memories of you
The days before our wedding
When you would sing for me under the shade of a tree
The way your hair turned golden in the sun
How your eyes were always full of passion, and love

Your face would flush with every compliment I gave
You're the only one keeping me grounded

Yet one day
After I awake on the cold floor of the room
The room I'm unable to escape
I can't picture your face
Your songs of forever, your songs of our future
I no longer know the words
As I panic, trying desperately to recall
I forget what it is I'm recalling
I can't remember why I missed you
Or who you were
Only one memory of my life remains
I am Eurydice
And I don't know who you were

# DAWN

JASHAN KAUR

Eerie silence.
Empty streets shrouded in darkness.
The world holding its breath, waiting...
The moment comes slowly.
Soft peachy hues fight their way onto the midnight blue sky,
leisurely mingling with mellow yellows.
Then, almost like magic, Life breathes into the silent world.
A golden sun lazily blooms over the horizon,
releasing an explosion of colour.
Its radiant rays gently graze the great greenery.
Songbirds serenade the new day,
their sweet melodies flowing through the crisp morning air.
People are abruptly awoken from their peaceful dreams,
groggily lured to the kitchen
with the rich scent of roasted coffee beans.
Chilly breezes filled with the pungent aroma
of flora brush past jovial school children,
emitting from them squeals of delight.

The thunderous rumbling of automobiles
soon overtakes the soothing sounds of nature.
Busy bees and curious critters
mimic their human counterparts,
preparing for a long day of work.
The day has truly begun.

# THE MISSING SCIENCE PARTNER

JACQUELINE TE KANI-NANKIVELL

Anne took the second to last lab coat from the hook beside the periodic table and put it on, looking around with a big smile. The chairs and tables were just like the ones at her old school, where science was her favourite class. Other students chatted away to their partners, lighting Bunsen burners. A stinging smell filled the room. Anne's face turned red when she realised she was the only one without a partner. She raised her hand.

"Where's my partner?" she said to Mrs Green, the teacher.

"Mel? She never comes to science class. Always has an excuse."

Anne was fed up. First off, the school was by a mouldy old cemetery, secondly all the hippy country kids were so rude and wouldn't help her on her first day, and to top it all off she had to start a science project by herself.

Without thinking, she stomped back to her table, bumping into it, knocking her glass beaker onto the floor. *Smash!* She heard laughter and whispers behind her.

Mrs Green handed her a brush and shovel.

"Clean it up," she said, with an angry tone to her voice.

This wasn't a good way to make a first impression as the new kid at school.


The floorboards of the corridor creaked as Anne dragged her feet to the cafeteria, her head down.

"See you around three-ish!" A girl yelled at someone down the other end of the corridor.

"Okay Mel," someone yelled back.

Anne looked up to see Mel walking backwards. She tried to step to the side but was too late – their heads clashed. *Bang!*

Mel helped Anne up.

"I'm sorry, are you okay? You want some ice or something?"

"It's okay but, weird question: why didn't you show up to science today?"

"What's it to you?"

"Because you're my science partner and you left me to do the work by myself!"

For a second Mel went from energetic to sad, looking down with a frown. She shook it off.

"'Cause I hate science and have better things to do," she said, and walked away.

Anne rubbed her chin.


Anne slipped on her lab coat and saw it was starting to get dark outside. She still had to catch up on her project.

Mrs Green said, "In half an hour I'll be packing up. See you then."

"This would be a lot easier if my partner was here," Anne said to herself as the teacher left.

Anne scrolled through Wikipedia on the science lab computer.

In the corner of her eye she saw a shadow move. At first, she assumed it was Mrs Green, so she kept doing her research. Then she looked over and saw a school girl with green hair trying to show her something written on a clipboard. Something about the girl put Anne off, and she looked down to see the girl's lab coat had no legs connecting her to the floor – she was floating. Looking back up, Anne saw the girl's face was as green as her hair.

Anne ran out of the room to Mrs Green.


Trophies behind glass sparkled in the sunshine coming through the window of the gym. Anne's class was warming up, running around the court as another class played basketball. Mel caught up to Anne, both of them sweaty and out of breath.

"I'd rather be in the cafeteria eating famous lasagne," Mel says.

Anne laughed, nodding.

"My mum tried to get me into badminton," she said, "but I hate it, which made me never want to do sports again."

"That sounds like my old science partner, she had a bad experience with sports too. She died her hair green to get back at her mum."

"Wait – green hair?"

"Yeah. Why do you say it like that?"

"Well ... I was finishing *our* homework, and I saw a schoolgirl with green hair and a lab coat on. She looked normal until I saw she didn't have feet, and I looked up and she had a green face."

"Don't make jokes about her like that," Mel said, raising her voice. Everyone turned their head to Mel.

The teacher told Mel to quiet down. She burst into tears and ran out of the gym.

Anne was confused. Out of breath, she focused on finishing her run.

After gym, Anne was curious to find out why Mel burst into tears. She zoomed over to the science lab, looking for answers. Brushing her hand along the dusty window frames, she wasn't really sure what she was looking for.

"May the ghost who haunts the corridors of this school come out and show me what I'm looking for."

"Anne! What are you doing?" a voice said.

Anne jumped, goosebumps all over her.

"Mrs Green! I thought you were a ghost!"

"You're looking for something?"

"Yes, I'm looking for info about last year's science class."

"Look over there, grab a yearbook."

Anne looked where the teacher was pointing. Next to a model skeleton there was a shelf with old school yearbooks. She skimmed through the previous year, looking for a picture of her friend. In the corner of her eye, she saw a photo of Mel and the girl with green hair – the same girl she saw as a ghost. Both were standing with a teacher she'd never seen before, with their lab coats on. Both had big watermelon smiles, posing with a dissected toad.

*I can't believe Mel lied about hating science,* Anne thought, *why would she lie to me?*

Anne strode back to Mrs Green.

"Who is this Mr. Harlem? Why did he leave?"

Mrs Green's voice was soft and shaky as she said, "since the incident last year, he's gone a bit haywire."

"What incident?"

"I'm not allowed to talk about it."

It was hard to track him down, but Anne found him. His house was a rundown old apartment on the wrong side of the tracks. Walking along his street, she passed graffitied walls and broken windows. A dog barked. Police sirens wailed. According to the yearbook, Mr. Harlem was the best-dressed teacher, and he really loved science. At his address, she saw a man drinking on the porch. He was wearing a stained white singlet with sweatpants and unmatched, holey socks. It looked like he hadn't brushed his hair in decades.

"Excuse me," Anne said, "do you know Levi Harlem?"

"Yes, present. What do you want?"

"Sorry, Mr Harlem, I didn't recognise you!"

"Are you one of my old students? I don't want anything to do with that school."

Mr Harlem turned to go inside the house, but Anne stopped him, "I've been seeing the ghost of Maggie in class!"

He walked back out.

"You must be crazy. There's no such thing as ghosts."

"Just tell me about Mel and Maggie and I'll go away."

"Oh, Maggie and Mel. They were such talented students. Definitely my favourites. So sad what happened to Maggie."

"What happened?"

"Didn't your teacher tell you?"

"Tell me what?"

"It was a failed science experiment that led to her death. My fault. I should never have left them alone." He skulled the rest of his beer. "They were trying to reverse rotting in food, cut down on food wastage. Maggie tested the formula. Ate a pear they had tested the formula on. Died.”

Anne's mouth fell open.

“That's so tragic! She was so young!”

“Yeah, so tragic. Now get off my property.”

Anne yanked Mel by the back of her sweatshirt.

“Are you crazy!?” Mel yelled. “What are you doing?”

Anne didn't hear a word, as the school bell ringing was so loud. She threw Mel into the science lab and slammed the door behind her.

“I know why you hate science so much! You should have just told me what happened!”

“You know nothing,” Mel said, “Maggie was my only friend and it was all my fault!”

“Why are you blaming yourself?”

“Because I was the one who was supposed to test the formula. Before I could grab it, Maggie snatched it and took a bite. She looked fine for the first five minutes, but then she turned green. By the time we got to the hospital, she had died.”

“But it wasn't your fault. She chose to eat it. She was the one who took the risk.”

The blinds rattled at the window and both girls turned as the lights flickered.

Over by the lab coats behind Mel, the girl with green hair floated as she put on one of the coats.

“Look,” Anne said, “it's Maggie.”

Mel frowned at Anne.

“This is a serious conversation, Anne, and here you are making jokes.”

"Seriously," Anne said, putting her hand on Mel's back to push her around to look.

Mel's hand went to her throat, and Anne saw her body stiffen.

"Maggie?"

The ghost smiled, saying, "Oh Mel, it's been so long. I've missed you so much."

Mel reached out for a hug, but her arms held onto nothing. She walked straight through Maggie.

Mel laughed as tears went down her cheeks.

"I should've been the one to test it. None of this would have happened."

"Get this through that small brain of yours, Mel: It's not your fault. Stop blaming yourself. I did what I did. There's nothing we can do now. You can't reverse my death."

Maggie went over to the whiteboard and explained what went wrong.

"All this time I've been dead I've figured out what went wrong. I want you to finish this off with Anne."

Maggie started to write a formula, filling up the entire whiteboard with numbers and equations. Mel started questioning her about it. Anne looked on, confused. Soon enough, she caught on to what the other two are talking about. It all came together.

"I'll do it," Mel said.

"You can't do it by yourself, that's why Anne is here to help you."

"No, I want to finish off what I started."

Anne's cheeks heated up. *Doesn't she trust me?*

"Please, Mel," Maggie said, "for my sake and yours, two heads are better than one and a ghost."

Mel sighed, then chuckled.

"Fine."

"Try not to mess it up."

"I'll try not to kill my next partner."

"I'm going to pretend I didn't hear that," Anne said.

The two girls copied Maggie's formula.

"Aha," Mel said, "that's what the problem was."

Mel picked the lock of the science cupboard, where all the hazardous chemicals were stored. Anne's hands were soon filled with very important stuff.

"This is a do-or-die science project, Anne, we can't miss a step."

At the metal bench, she measured a green liquid into a beaker, then mixed in a white powder.

As the sun rose, Mel said, "We're done, we've cracked it!"

They rushed to the cafeteria. It was still early in the morning, so the lights were off and the room was cold. Anne shivered.

Mel ran to the bucket of pig scraps behind the counter.

"Ew, I don't wanna touch this!"

"Look here, you wimp!" Anne pulled out a rotten sandwich, covered with green fuzzy mould.

"Wow, impressive," Mel said. She grabbed the spray bottle and sprayed the sandwich.

The process took a few minutes. The sandwich went from mouldy and stinky to a fresh, bakery-bought sandwich.

Anne hesitated, then with a wobbly voice said, "I'll do it."

"No," Mel said, grabbing the sandwich from Anne, "I'll do it, it's the right thing to do. For Maggie's sake."

Mel took a big bite, with her fingers crossed. She struggled to swallow, her eyes scrunched up. Her eyes popped, her eyebrows raised.

"Wow! This is delicious!"

Anne entered the science lab.

"You're late, Anne," Mrs Green said. Mel walked in.

"Mel? I never thought you'd come back."

"Long time no see, Mrs Green."

"No time wasting, go grab a lab coat and find you and your partner a seat."

Anne reached over to grab the second to last coat, and Mel grabbed the last one.

Butterflies fluttered in Anne's stomach as she realised this was the first time she'd had a lab partner since she came to this school. She hugged Mel, who made gagging noises.

"Ew, I'm a lone wolf."

"Not anymore. You have me."

Mel looked around the class, then turned to a seat that had been empty a moment before. She saw her old lab partner, Maggie, smiling at her. She tapped Anne on the shoulder.

"Really? Your first class and you're not paying attention."

"Look!"

Anne turned, as Maggie slowly disappeared.

"So long, Anne, take care of Mel."

A happy tear slid down Anne's cheek. She knew she and Mel would be friends for a long time.

# I AM FROM

## MOANA HOOGLAND

I am from
summer days of endless writing
an ocean's worth of hope
a dreamers love of life
imaginative scope

I am from
ballet dancing childhood
tap dancers' tiptoe shoes
gymnastic twists and jumps
fantastic hairdos

I am from
sulky teenage tantrums
several years of moods
a large, noisy family
laughter and real food

I am from
a warm, humble house
in a small, unnoticed land
trying to make my name
with the pen held in my hand.

# THE MASK

HOLLY FLYGER

What secrets do those eyes keep?
How much pain does she conceal behind a smile?
If only someone could listen to her tales,
then maybe she wouldn't take the leap.

The unheard thoughts will forever be lost.
Unhealed scars will remain in her soul.
Even now no one can see behind her mask,
where she hides all her pains from the world.

# THE WRONGS OF THE MARSHLANDER

## ROMAN SEATON

*Wiler was a troubled man with a troubled mind.*

The fog lights streamed over the winding road. A rush of salted froth from the coast crashed against the cliffside road. Thick tendrils of moss swayed below crooked branches. Squinting through the darkness, Wiler made out the steep road snaking away before him, away from the sea and into the marsh. The car made a turn, the spinning wheels spitting up chunks of wet, cold mud.

His old Plymouth sped up, skimming down the reserve at breakneck speed. The wind whipped at the fog lights. Mist clouded the windscreen and Wiler craned his neck out the side window in an attempt to see the road ahead. Quickly, he ducked his head back in, each passing branch intent on decapitating him. Well into the darkest hour, the dim flare of the fog lights failed as the mist thickened. Sweat spread across Wiler's face. The trees grew taller, blocking out the moon's light and casting down shadows of grotesque skeletal fingers in the midnight fog. He did not have much time.

Wiler heard a click. A flash of light tore into his retina. Blinded, he tried the brakes, but the old Plymouth kept speeding down the slope. His vision cleared just in time to see the crash barrier. The steel railings split apart, sending the mud-clad car cartwheeling over the cliffside. The whole world seemed to slow down, and in an instant, time stopped.

Glass shattered, blood burst, metal creaked and Wiler's neck snapped forward. Shattered glass rained down like hail, bouncing off the broken bonnet. An all-consuming fog pulled at his eyes, sending an eerie coldness through his skull. His neck cracked forwards, his head hitting the ripped dashboard and he dropped into the deep moors of unconsciousness

*Footsteps.*

Wiler opened his eyes. It hurt to open his eyes. He winced and pulled himself from the wreckage. His head swam. His briefcase was torn to pieces and he reached back to take it. His bruised fingers made purchase, but his sore back protested. He pulled harder, tears in his eyes. He searched the case, rummaging through the remains. He felt the cool supple plastic of the binder and he removed it from his tattered case. The documents were still intact. He sucked the blood off his fingers, as he felt the thick squelching earth beneath a shoeless foot. Wiler gazed upwards towards the night sky, desperate for some sense of safety in the marshes.

*Why did he come here? Just to see a grayed old crank who couldn't afford a second-rate swamp anymore? But he needed this, he needed this money, even if his client was a murderer.* All he needed was a signature on the deeds. To meet the land owner at dawn on the edge of the marsh. *So why did life have to be so damn hard?* he thought, and not for the first time in recent months. Maybe even years.

He'd just lost his car and had nearly lost his life. *How would you explain that?*

He looked up through his tears, the hairs on his neck prickling, he sensed he was not alone. A ruined gravel road split through the swamp. He heard movement. He wandered from the wreckage of his car. Wiler listened again and heard ... footsteps.

He peered around, but the tall blackened trees made it near impossible to see anything. Wiler craned his neck behind him, and through the mist he saw a crooked figure. Wiler knew what to expect of the man, his client had explained: a stubborn old man reluctant to let go of his family land.

The old man stood still; his face turned away. Wiler moved towards the figure, trudging across the gravel, hissing and huffing as his stinging wounds bled onto the road. Everything hurt. A metre from the shape, Wiler opened his mouth to speak, but his dry throat afforded only a series of harsh rasping coughs.

After a long empty silence, he tried again.

"H-hello, sir," Wiler said, trying to hide his informality, "are you the land owner? I am here to represent my client. I believe that you have been expecting me."

The silhouette turned around. "Yes ..."

A tall thin man dressed in black, a briefcase in one hand. The man seemed almost skeletal, with long skinny arms and a heavy black coat. He craned down towards Wiler's face. He was too close, too close for comfort.

"And you would be the lawyer?"

His lips spat out the sentence. He frowned down at Wiler, the corners of the man's face seemed pulled at the edges, with his greyed pale skin almost corpse-like.

"Yes, my name is Wiler. I've been sent here to act as intermediary for the land transfer--"

The land owner cut him off. "The documents, Mr Lawyer."

From his coat pocket, the skeletal man drew a bony hand. His outstretched fingers opened and closed inches from Wiler's face.

"Oh yes, the documents," Wiler stammered.

Wiler opened the binder, peeling away the plastic edges. He hissed as he pulled out the deeds. Wiler paused before he handed over the papers. He felt uncomfortable, something about this man, about this ... *place*. It all seemed to be going too fast, something wasn't right.

The man's hand hung frozen, hungry. Then he said, "Thank you, Mr Lawyer."

Somehow the skeletal man already held the deeds, sliding them into his crimson briefcase. With an effort Wiler regained his composure.

"Thank you for being so cooperative. It's been good doing business with you, I cannot thank you enough Mr ...?" *What was his name?* Wiler thought, but his mind had gone blank.

The skeletal man smiled, his dead empty grin stretched at its corners, revealing a set of blackened chalky teeth. His smile was too big for his mouth, he seemed so ... *Synthetic,* Wiler thought.

"My name is Pagvol ... Pagvol Marsher." And with a nod of his head, he turned around.

Wiler looked at his empty hand. Typically, the lawyer takes the documents on behalf of the client. He shouldn't, really, be handing papers to the client like this. His mind told him that he should object, say something at least. But by the time Wiler looked up Pagvol was gone, and he only made out his silhouette as he faded into the mist.

By the time Pagvol disappeared, Wiler didn't understand why he was scared of the man in the first place. *He's just a creepy old man who wants a decent retirement plan,* he told himself.

But something else nagged at him. Why would anyone choose to buy a place like this? No car could get through these marshes without being either lost, or turned into a crash site. *How did Pagvol get here?*

The mist began to lift, and squinting, Wiler saw the early morning sun rising over the mountain ranges. The sunlight hit the old road, illuminating his way back to the settlement. Barefoot, hurting and troubled by doubts scratching at the back of mind, Wiler picked his way over the rough concrete, inching along the marshland highway. Wiler had finished the job, he could afford her ring now, if she would even pick up the phone or talk to him.

All he needed was to get home, to find his car and get away from this place and drown out the memories of the deed.


Smelling the smoke, Wiler turned ...

Ahead, there was a ruined car on the road, the bonnet smouldering and the engine blown. Wiler's mind screamed in protest, every instinct told him to run, but he carried on walking. Wiler kept moving towards the vehicle, stumbling, sick with vomit and mud dripping down his chin. Heart pounding, Wiler peered inside the car to find it barren of life, nobody.

His fingers fumbled at the door, tugging at the handle. *Locked, of course it was locked.*

The wrecked car in shreds, bullet holes in the tires, it was hopeless, he had gone too far, it was time to turn around. And then he touched it ... a cold wet tingling in the sole of his foot, soon an icy chill, began to make its way up his leg, sending tremors through his spine.

*Blood.*

The morning sun shone pale through the mist, but Wiler didn't need to look to know what he was standing in ... blood, the car stank of the stuff. Looking down at his bare feet, his fears were confirmed, a thick red mess trailed across the road, curving towards the half-open boot of the car.

*A briefcase.* Wiler's mind screamed, but he didn't know why.

The wrecked car's headlights were still on, he could see the briefcase. He shuffled through the fog. Wiler rocked to and fro, cradling it in his arms. Twisting the metal, Wiler realised it was locked. Swearing under his breath, Wiler smashed the lock against the tailgate. A crack began to form on the case's lid. *Progress,* Wiler said to himself. Straining his arms, Wiler lifted the case into the air, and brought it down hard against the metal. The lock snapped and the mangled hinges cracked backwards, the case's contents spilled across the gravel.

Scratched sheets of paper drifted down onto the concrete road.

Wiler stared at the papers, as a sense of familiarity began to dawn on him. The floodgates opened, memories streamed into his mind. Wiler clutched at his head, white hot pain throbbing through his brain, penetrating it like little needles.

*He never delivered the papers, Wiler never left the crash, he never delivered the ...*

"The papers ... "

Wiler straightened, briefcase in hand he stumbled down into the marshes. He walked for what seemed hours, or was it minutes? He stopped as a thin bony silhouette took form from the mist. Wiler stared at the shape, the skeletal man turned towards him. The deformed, otherworldly angles of the man's face seemed almost familiar to him, but yet alien and unknowable.

"Give me the papers, Wiler."

The skeletal man's eyes darted towards his folder, expectant, waiting for something.

"Oh yes, the documents," Wiler muttered.

Wiler drew the papers from the folder. His mind told him to stop, but his body stiffened as he placed them into the man's open hand. He did not know this man; he had never known this man in his life. But a same nagging sense of familiarity tugged at his mind, a single half-formed name boiled at the back of Wiler's head.

"Thank you, Wiler."

The skeletal man grinned a dead, empty smile, needle-like teeth protruding from the gums of his mouth. Through the fog, Wiler could almost see what appeared to be stitches running along the edges of the man's face. With a nod of his head, the skeletal man slowly faded into the mist.

*Marsher, Pagvol Marsher. That was his name.* Wiler was there to represent his client. Pagvol was expecting him.

By the time Pagvol disappeared, Wiler didn't understand why he was scared of the man in the first place. *He's just a creepy old man who wants a decent retirement plan,* he told himself.

Wiler smiled. All he needed to do was to go home now, to find his car and get away from this place and drown out the memories of the deed.

# PART 6

# POETRY



Poetry can be described as a rhythmic interplay of words, style, stanza or verse. Often poetry will appeal to an emotional response from the reader or challenge them to delve deeper into thought about a particular topic or theme. Some poems may shock, while others are simply an observation or thought about a moment in time. In this segment of the book, a cross-section of poets from Tairāwhiti capture the essence of diversity in thought and form, while weaving words together to celebrate the love of language.

# WAKA AMA WAHINE KARAKIA

KAREN MORRIS-DENBY

E Tangaroa manaakitia tēnei hoe ki runga i te wai Turanganui
E Tāwhirimātea
kia tau ngāhau e whā
kia tau te hau ki muri
Ki a mātou tīpuna e whakahōnore
Tēna koe mò ngā painga o tēnei rā mīharo

We ask you Tangaroa for your blessing as we paddle
on the waters of Tūranganui
We call upon Tāwhirimātea to calm all winds
East West North and South
Allow us to have a peaceful wind to follow us
We honour our ancestors
We give thanks for the blessings you have bestowed upon us
On this wonderful day

# WAKA AMA WAHINE

KAREN MORRIS-DENBY

Listen to the gentle whisper of a Karakia through the air
And feel the gentle caress
of the sea guardian through your hair
Your Silhouettes slowly glide across the morning horizon line
With the beauty of the moment an image called divine
The white gulls circle around you through the breaking dawn
The pastel colours of sunlight reflect the sorrows
since Earth was born
The sounds of waiting waters grow louder with every step

As you all shoulder your sleek burden
many secrets are well-kept
The waka ama is lowered like a child that's in your care
Then the rhythm of the paddles, a sensual elegance you revere
All the troubles of each life are left upon the shores
With each 'hup' you stoically follow like an unspoken law
The spirits of the ocean surround
each of you wahine like a cloak

The feeling of elation can never be felt by landlubber folk
Once you return to your families
and everything appears the same
You remember you stroked the son of Papatuanuku,
Tangaroa is his name.

# HAIKU

## KAREN MORRIS-DENBY

Musket fire horror
Through the stillness of the dawn
Poverty for Cook

Cliffs white as Dover
Nick's 'Ahoy' still echoing
Salute to the sun

Māori souls still weep
Cook can never turn the past
Grey sands stories hold

Voices on the wind
Whispering along the sands
Gisborne's secrets past

Silence fills the air
Echoing around the bay
Lost souls remembered

# TICKING

PHILOMENA MCGANN

If time measured love
Instead of hours
hearts would not cease
Sun would set embraces
Moon would light belief

The clock could not tick
its seconds
Childs' play not end or chase
old couple's smiling presence
Young lovers full intense

The garden grows unfettered
by chiming of a knell
each tree and mountain climbing
the ocean tide and swell

Second instances of feeling

milliseconds of sublime
Creation fettered not by motion
sand is shifting, seeds will climb

Peoples, melting into moment
hearts sinking in the sun
Stars gaze to blaze the darkness
Creator sighs and all is done

# CELESTIAL BODY

## PHILOMENA MCGANN

By night our wishes spray upwards to the sky
and cloak the night in bright sparklers
Shooting stars of passionately felt emotions, hope and dreams
Flocking birds looking for rest and peace
Not rockets seeking revenge

Our wishes glimmer in the sky and like the planets can slowly die
Constant streams flying and we're all trying
To retain belief in good that triumphs
Telling each other happy tales of days gone by
Avoiding the newspapers' doom and terror

Light up the sky with laughter and
teach the young to honour life and love
Parade the streets to ask for justice
Hum lullabies to babes
Shine hope into the darkest shadows
Grasp the weak, clasp and speak not harsh but welcome words

Thank our lucky stars – or thank the powers – just remember to
say we are grateful

Remember our loved ones who left earth's shores
Slumbering or shining in the night sky
Surely they'll place their wishes next to ours and tenderly entreat
with prayers
Not headlines but heart lines, tracing palms cupped outward
evermore

Take my hand, I'll lead you safely once more
I am the stargazer that gathers them all into the net and uses their
blazened
brightness
To quell the evil dwelling darkness seekers –
Not completely, but enough … rest and trust

# ODE TO ONEROA

KATRINA REEDY

I step light upon you, beloved boardwalk, this daily return journey, from Waikanae to Midway, brief and breathtaking.

I waste no time, as footfall follows footfall, my lifeline weaving once again into the festival of motion upon your way.

Behind me now, joggers quickly gain ground. I step quietly to the left to make room as they pass.

A group at a picnic table, open up their fish & chips. The squeeze of all sauces onto newsprint, straight cut fries dipping in.

Up ahead, a man is getting dragged down to the water by his very happy pooch. Who owns who in this scene?

Further along a skateboarder joins the music of the day with a rumbling along the planks, thundering toward, then receding.

Goldfinch and sparrow dart ahead of me, mimicking the pilot boats, that guide the logging ships into the wharf.

To the right, the Norfolk pines stand ever watchful over you, assuring, shading. Their shadows stripe across you to the dunes.

I imagine a rocket launching at nearby Māhia. I pause to stretch, dipping low then reaching skyhigh.

To the left, the lush back dunes a splendid backdrop for shy lilies nestling in pairs, like lovers at the altar of the eloping.

I journey on past the Whispering Sands, net curtains billowing out like wedding veils, the perfect venue for a honeymoon.

At Roberts Road, surf school is underway and a family sits on the wide bench, up the gentle rise, watching on,

Cheering goes up as a novice goes from belly to grinning crouch in a well-timed catch of picture-perfect wave.

At Beacon reserve, twin kites soar, dancing in the wind as they are expertly constrained, they provoke the sky, searching, seeking.

A work ute pulls into the last empty carpark, just to stop for a bit, a long overdue break in a busy working week.

Only the few emerge from their vehicles. The lunchtime drive-in crowd content to enjoy the view from the privacy of their cars.

A pāharakeke flourishes to my right and to my left pīngao and wīwī giggle in the breeze.

At Midway beach a digger is on the sands removing lingering debris, restoring the sands, revealing history.

Time to head back, and I decide to leave the comfort of my beloved boardwalk, to head back, barefoot, along the sand.

As I head down to the shore the *Tairāwhiti* waka hourua pulls out into the bay. A magnificent sight upon calm teal waters!

Perhaps this was how the Horouta waka appeared upon arrival from Hawaiki, making land at Muriwai where pipi bathe and pāpaka scuttle.

Thoughts turn to Hinehākirirangi, the cultivator of kūmara upon Manawarū, Nurturer of her people, Bestower of the name 'Oneroa'.

She is the reason why you, my beloved boardwalk, exists up above the back dunes of her shores.

You are her invitation to journey, back into the past, to help the past teach the present to be brave, hardworking and nurturing.

Waiata of wahine toa carry me back to the carpark outside the entrance of Captain Morgan's.

As I leave, I catch a glimpse of mother and child heading off along Oneroa Boardwalk.

The child surging happily ahead, his mother trying hard to keep up.

# MOOBS

## CHRISTOPHER MCMASTER

i was driving over a
mountain pass late
one summer
stopping at the summit
to look at the valley
far below
clouds were racing past
close enough to touch
and one did
catching on an outcrop of rock
and the piece of cloud
that was torn off
clung while it could
a piece of cloud caught
in the mountain's grasp.

that was a MOOB
i said

one in my collection
a
Moment Of Outstanding Beauty.

the unspoken silence lingered
between us for a few moments.
then she smiled and said,
i've collected a couple of those
in the last few days.

and we left it at that.

# DEAD POETS SOCIETY

CHRISTOPHER MCMASTER

**bukowski is still dead**

you've got some trajectory
you hit my neck
she said

i stole those lines
but i asked first
then she smeared it on my chest
and licked her fingers

bukowski is dead
and the *Rialto*
waxes poetic

she writes
with economy

each word
so dense
with memory
and meaning

like a kernel of popcorn

i want to fry her
in oil
and watch
her burst

damn
that would taste good

but bukowski is still dead

he can't even
eat popcorn
now

**alan**

ginsberg wanted to clean his ass
but his lover liked it dirty

i saw him on tv and fell in love

with what was coming out of his
mouth

and his soul

its glow
filled the screen

his exit was the best
golden
with friends
and monks
and film crew

i want to die like that

# HEEMI TE WHATU APATARI (JIM POROU) REG.NO 817740

KATARINA POROU

for my mokopuna

'You're far too young!' they said
So off I went to Palmy
Enlisting in my mother's name ...
My pride in Muriwai!

'Your country needs you!' was the cry
So, young and fit we scrambled
'One and all must serve!' they called
'To fight for all our freedom'

Six long years we fought that war
Italy, Egypt and in Greece ...
Japan and in Pacific too ...
We marched 'C' Company

Our guns ablaze and bayonets drawn
Saw blood and guts and sickly stench
My mates one day ... and gone the next
'Oh mum, what hell is this!'

I find it hard to talk, moko ...
It's locked up here ... in my head
Some nights those demons reappear
When I'm not looking ... or in bed

So once again I'm on attack'
'Damn you ghostly shadows!'
I make my way to the RSA ...
Comrades drown our sorrows

We fought a war, not ours, moko
So that you'd be free
Returned with wounds you could not see
To pick up where we started

So we sang and laughed and reminisced
And told the mischief tales
Got on with life as best we could
In a world where much had changed

I hope you never have to fight a war
Your future resolute

My heart salutes you, moko ...
Grandpa/Koro Jim

# WHAIWHAIA

### KATARINA POROU

Coastie mates
Black gym pleats
Bedpress clothes

Shellite Iron
Tilly lamp
Candlestick

Long drop lav
Pine tree wind
Generator pump

Skinny mother
Flagon sherry
Sliding cupboard

Moemoea
Kupu whakaari

Sunday Ra

Bad spirit time
Fireball marked
Whaiwhaia

Gut-wrench mask
Churning heart
Protect kids

Karakia hard
Bless-ed wai
Eye to eye

Crawling tears
Guitar cuzzies
Soultime hymns

Song heart love
Third-eye strong
Pure child save

# DAWN

JESSICA KEAST

Take my breath, and throw it down wind
Let the breeze whisper, why am I here
The undulating waves soothe my thoughts,
My melancholy is smothered by salted air

One, two and three; you came to me and we came with you
I flood with fear, I drown in gratitude
At the edge of the world, stepping up to the sun
Why must my heart beat with the incessant sound of failure

If I plant my heart seeds in this sand,
Will my soul bloom and grow and flourish
Breathe new life into old bones
Sparkling turquoise depths engulf my lungs

I will ground myself down, to rise again new
Let luminous dawn trickle onto this open wound
I greedily consume the abundant lush air

And so, it heals not festers, it loves not falters

The exhilaration of love bared
This final stop on the brink of eternity
Illuminate my force and will, the fate and the stars
I lift and I soar, fresh future being

# HAIKU

## JO TITO

kōwhai yellow
seeded in a gentle earth
tui calls

remembering
heart beats of ancient ones
medicinal earth

# HEAVY

BENITA KAPE

It's rain heavy, heavier than heavy.
All is heavy in such rain's control
and insolence.

Scoured the hills last week;
Scours them again today.
Was anything left on those hills
of what they call *forestry slash?*
Left lying there, pretending that
exotic debris is the gold of renewal.
Tawhirimatea is offering fair warning.
His mother will have a say in this.

*Slash!* Biblical sliding, washed down the hills;
a ballet of logs, no one applauding:
valleys that could not hold
against the torrents, aggradations
whisper of hillsides that mount

in the rivers and ocean to clog
underneath. Rivers, shores, homes
and school ground layered with this mess.
Log ballet backups pack up for kilometres.
Slack, slipshod, slapdash, offhand and sloppy.

Forestry managers could you not foresee
the choreography? *laissez-faire* and casual as if
the problem doesn't belong to you.
Slack, slipshod, slapdash, offhand, sloppy.

Last week the rain, heavy, heavy.
The hills! What have they this time
to share? The heavy rain hammers, heave winds
her heavy front: left with a contractor's nightmare.
Slack, slipshod, slapdash, offhand, sloppy.

But I'll weep again for my apology. Thirty
years on from Cyclone Bola. Trees may push
their roots to the moon; this is ecos' ballet
not slack, slipshod, slapdash, offhand, sloppy
*forestry slash.*

# CERAMIC

*(HALCYON SANCTA – DARK MANTRA)*

BENITA KAPE

Why such a stunning bird on a background
of black, all colour in his grand plumage
drawn down? We can find no relief in the
in the feathers of blue that might catch our
eye; the slow hovering that hints
at a flakiness from the soul of the clay;
the artist's endeavour not to reveal
something that intrudes and
intrudes with no hint of sky.

King-fisher;
whose awesome beauty became
the tinkling sound of ceramic
heavily striking solid ground.
A harmony of shards,
apposite and quick.

# PART 7

# SPECULATIVE AND SCIENCE FICTION

Speculative fiction addresses human themes from the perspective of a world that is a little stranger than the one we live in. In *Bitter Pill*, Janine Hamilton-Kells looks at aging, and an ultimate solution, freeing up resources for others. In *Journey to the Stars*, Christopher McMaster tells of a man chasing aliens who finally gets what he (thought he) wanted. *Dreamscape*, by Claire Price, is more heavenly, an experience in a higher dimension, a surreal trip of sense and sensuality. Aaron Compton examines where the old meets the new, in a world where the synthetic intellects of powerful machines have stolen the personas of our atua and gods, in *Grow Me Some Wings*. *Maiden Flight*, by Dorothy Fletcher, tells of a young woman on a savage journey of self-discovery and transformation.

# A BITTER PILL

JANINE HAMILTON-KELLS

The knock on the door was perfunctory, as if they knew she was home. They probably did, thought Edith, anxiety fluttering in her belly. She knew they had ways. Edith knew of people who had tried to avoid this moment by having no fixed address, by travelling endlessly as if to outpace the inevitable. It never worked. Edith reached to unlatch the door, her hand looked weathered, her knuckles swollen, age spots spreading like splattered paint across her skin. Perhaps it was time after all.

Her throat felt dry as she opened the door. The sunlight streamed into the balcony and silhouetted the man and woman standing in their tasteful streetwear.

"Ms Edith Forey?"

"Yes," said Edith, hating the slight tremor in her voice.

"Fingerprint here please, Edith."

Edith stared at them for a moment. Her hand shook slightly as she held a finger against the screen, activating the courier receipt.

They handed her the box. It looked ordinary and she turned without saying goodbye, a small snub but a victory nonetheless.

She knew they didn't see her as a person. As the child who had adored her older brother and loved each of her pets with devotion. As the girl who fell in love too easily, the mother who had tried to hold her child too close for too long, or the wife that had felt too much resentment to stay married. She had been a gardener and still was if you could count the contraband flowers on her windowsill, each vying for a sliver of afternoon sun.

For the rest of the afternoon, the box seemed to glow like a beacon, no matter where in the small flat she placed it. She wondered if she should call someone, but felt conspicuous, as if they were waiting to see what she would do. It had started with clever media campaigns, a loosening of euthanasia laws, 'death with dignity' had become a catchphrase. The marketing machine was superb, clever advertising rolling out, littered with words like empowered, sacrifice and choice.

In the end, it had all come down to a pill. Issued to every citizen turning seventy, arriving by signed courier during the week of your birthday. It was up to each person when to take it, or that was the plan. At first, the pill had seemed civilised and empowering, people were giddy with it, as if they had received some kind of newfound freedom or hard-won right. Living funerals became all the rage, 'Live Fast, Die Young!' was graffitied on building walls. Edith had always suspected that these slogans were part of the government propaganda. No Banksy at work there, thought Edith.

Edith felt a heightened awareness and wondered if it was adrenaline she could feel coursing through her body, or maybe cortisol. She had always gotten the two mixed up but seemed to remember that one of them gave you belly fat. As if that matters now, she thought, perhaps I should increase my trans fats, who needs a pill?

She glanced again at the box, feeling as if she should lock it away, even though she knew from the briefing that it could only be opened with her fingerprint. Suddenly decided, she grabbed her coat and the plaid scarf that had once been her father's and left the apartment, pulling the door shut firmly behind her. She walked determinedly to the stairs, holding the handrail as she descended, to combat the shaky feeling she still carried. As she reached the community gardens below, she scouted the lawn for Deirdre.

Deirdre had a way about her, an unflappable quality that Edith needed. She was working amongst a small group, picking snow peas in the hydroponic beds. With one look at Edith's face, she knew that the delivery had happened. Deirdre approached, arms outstretched, her soft arms gathering her friend to her chest. She rested her chin gently on Edith's greying hair and for a moment Edith relaxed into the comfort, her usual reserve slipping away, before drawing back embarrassed.

"Everyone will know. It's so public. I'm now just a relic, a product past its use-by." Edith looked at Deirdre, her cheeks coloured with shame.

"Chin up. Even though we know it's going to happen it still comes as a shock. You'll get through it."

"I know, I know. It's just so official. Like someone has set a timer for the end of my life and I can hear it ticking." Deirdre watched her for a moment with that gaze she had, so calm and accepting.

"Come to the group tonight," she urged. "It helps to connect with others who have experienced it. The Boxers we call ourselves now, it makes us feel like we're fighters, empowered, that's what we were fed after all wasn't it?" Deirdre smiled.

Edith managed a tight smile in return.

"I might," she said. "Maybe not tonight, but soon, when I get more used to it. I think I'll head down to the canal for a bit." Edith backed away with an awkward wave, the warmth and comfort she had felt against Deirdre's chest already fading like a dream.

As she neared the canal, a wave of growing anger rose from her gut like an acidic tide. She thought of the years her generation had fought for freedom of speech, pay and gender equality, for safety, irrespective of faith, ethnicity or sexual orientation. And for what?

Edith passed a group of hooded young men. They didn't acknowledge her; she had become invisible. The canals were a CCTV zone and Edith had an almost irrepressible urge to pull the finger at the camera.

She paused at a break in the Perspex tunnels that ran alongside the canal; the tunnels, like the pill, had been one of the government's ideas to improve quality of life. Clean and brilliant when first installed, they were now tired and deserted, acting as a barrier to the water rather than a way to connect with it. The stench of urine and rotting leaves deterred all but the most stubborn walkers. Edith stopped and looked into the grey canal water. Life had never taken off in the way she had hoped. She hadn't imagined her senior years in this tenement block, alone with the plants on her windowsill. She wondered who would water her plants when she was gone. I may as well stop watering them now, she thought. What's the point in prolonging it? She grimaced as it dawned on her that this was the very attitude that people now have toward the ageing population. The irony wasn't lost on her, but it was no comfort.

She thought of all the plans she had as a girl, the opportunities lost, and the experiences she had planned for her 'bucket list.'

A vulgar expression, thought Edith, shaking her head in disgust. She remembered looking in her bathroom mirror on her fortieth birthday feeling saddened by the signs of ageing reflected back at her. The laugh lines, the softening skin on her eyelids, the beginnings of soft jowls around her jawline. Ridiculous, she thought, I was so young and so beautiful then. I should have done all those things that were frowned upon. I should have danced until dawn, gotten a tattoo and kissed a man with a beard. Edith felt a yearning tight in her chest; she had almost forgotten kissing. The brief moment she had just shared with Deirdre was the most physical contact she had had in too many years to count.

The clouds seemed to darken, the cold wind biting through Edith's thin coat. She turned to go back to the complex, her flat, and the box that it held. Nobody was in the garden when she returned. In truth, there was not enough space there for growing much at all. Reaching her flat, Edith couldn't shake the feeling of being watched. She felt conspicuous. As the door swung open, she noticed three slips of paper on the linoleum that had been pushed under the door. She didn't recognise the writing and, as she read them, tears blurred her vision. One was a family asking to be considered for her flat in the ballot, a recommendation from the existing resident can advance an application. The second was a leaflet for cremation caskets, the third a scrawled note with the simple words: "Don't be an oxygen thief!"

Edith felt a surge of adrenaline. The vultures were circling, this was how it started; would she be able to withstand the pressure, to justify her existence? Edith turned to the empty corridor outside.

"It's supposed to be my choice!" she shouted. "My choice! When I'm ready!"

Sobbing, she slammed the door, fingers shaking, she screwed up the offending notes and threw them across the floor. She scanned the room, eyes coming to rest on the box. I can't stand this, she thought. With shaking hands, she shoved the box into the cupboard below her tiny sink. Dragging her armchair to the window farthest from the cupboard she faced it out toward the sky. As she sank into the chair, Edith was overcome with exhaustion, a fatigue so bone-wearingly deep that she was paralysed by it. She spent the night staring out of the window watching the sky darken, and then many hours later, the sun peeking through the haze, shining in broken tangents through the cityscape. As the sun rose so did Edith's determination, a spark of something she didn't recognise rising from her gut. She was tired of being downtrodden, of doing what others expected.

"I'm going nineties," she smiled. "I choose life!"

Edith crossed the complex, this time with purpose and resolve, raising her chin in the air and eyeballing the CCTV cameras. She soon reached her destination in a part of town she didn't normally frequent. She grasped the handle of the shop door with her weathered hand and had a brief flashback to the previous day when she had opened the door to the delivery. It seemed like more than twenty-four hours had passed. She faltered and then with a determined push she entered the tattoo parlour. An elfin girl with auburn hair looked up from her instruments.

"I'm here for a tattoo," Edith said, challenging the girl with her eyes.

"Sure thing," the girl said. "You know that excludes you from certain medical insurances, right?"

"Yes, I know and I don't care."

The girl raised an eyebrow, suppressing a smirk. "Well, hop on up then. What tattoo were you thinking of?"

"I want a date," Edith said. "Yesterday's date to be exact, and make it look like a barcode."

"A barcode?"

"Yes, you remember those, don't you? Here on my bicep where people will see it." Edith gestured to her arm.

The tattoo artist set to work scanning an image she created on her device. "Hold still," she instructed as she began to tattoo Edith's tiny arm. She looked up as she felt Edith flinch, to see Edith's eyes watering, lips clenched with steely resolve.

"Fancy listening to some music?" she asked.

"Sure," Edith agreed.

The tattooist waved her hand over a speaker and the room filled with the incongruous sound of reggae beats. "You listen to Bob Marley?" asked Edith.

"Sure, I do," said the girl who couldn't be more than twenty-five. "It's old school, I like the lyrics."

Edith leaned back closing her eyes, her racing heart slowing to the beat of Bob Marley's *One Love, One Heart*. For a moment in that tired tattoo parlour, Edith and the young tattooist shared a moment of synchronicity, a quiet acknowledgement of shared human experience, to the sounds of a reggae singer preaching love and unity. Without realising it, they both hummed along to the chorus.

"You're done," said the artist a few moments later, as she wiped a strong-smelling cloth over Edith's arm.

"You know, we do get a few of you in here, just after. We even thought of running a bucket list special for a while."

"I hate that expression," said Edith. "I have more stuff to do than would fill a buckct."

The girl smiled as if really seeing Edith for the first time. "Why the barcode?" she asked. Edith looked at her, a smile brushing her lips.

"I'm embracing the idea of being expired. Every day I live past my use-by date I become more dangerous to consume." The girl threw her head back laughing and Edith joined her, her laugh feeling rusty, but coming from the same place that the humming had come from.

# JOURNEY TO THE STARS

## CHRISTOPHER MCMASTER

Tom chased aliens like others chased storms. He chased them for the same reasons too. He met a group once, or rather, their paths crossed. Wild eyes and messy hair, they were more excited the closer they got to their storm. They obviously lived for it. He wasn't all that different from them – he was just as excited, just as wild-eyed, just as crazed the closer he got. On that occasion, he watched them peel away as the storm continued to move. They didn't understand why Tom didn't follow as the storm tracked west, but he wasn't interested in any terrestrial meteorological event. He was after what, or who, was hiding behind it. He *knew* something was there.

Just like the storm chasers followed their leads, Tom followed his. There were lots of leads to pick up on. Short wave radio was his favourite. It was awash in theorists, or conspiracists, and chasers like himself. And it was immediate. There was no delay in uploading files, no hours wasted in trolling websites or following endless paths with keywords for breadcrumbs. Tom prided himself in reading between the lines, in seeing relevant data in observations that the person on air didn't even see. He was also adept at picking out the plants, the hoaxers, paid by the government or whoever, to redirect the gaze, to sow some confusion. There was that place in America, what they called 'Area 51'. Now there *was* a conspiracy, just not the one a lot of people believed. Classic redirection. Simple, but effective. If you get people looking in one place, they aren't looking where they should.

Tom didn't care who paid them, the plants and hoaxers, or why they did it. He ignored their noise and listened for ... *authentic* leads. It was that kind of information that led to meeting the storm chasers. He caught a few adjectives in a broadcast, a few geographical descriptors, headed to where he thought was mentioned, talked to a few locals. Hearsay is usually like gold dust, leading to a richer vein. He drove into the outback, lied to the storm freaks, and flanked the cloud bank they were following.

He saw them that time, if only a glimpse. The lights. Coordinated, intelligent lights.

By that point in time, he was already down the rabbit hole. He sold whatever belongings he had, quit his dead-end job, traded his rudderless life for a rugged old Ford with a camper shell over the bed and a shortwave radio. Stocked with water, a camp stove, a couple boxes of two-minute noodles and a sleeping bag, he was self-sufficient. Whenever a promising lead cropped up, he chased it. He could relocate to the new hotspot, triangulate his data, and be there. Waiting.

He waited on this night. He drove the Ford as far he could and left it parked by a ravine. He hiked through the gully, across more desert, and climbed a hill, the highest point in the vicinity. He looked to the north. All his data pointed north. And he waited, studying the night sky. He saw Orion reach up and across the expanse. In the New Mexican night sky, Orion stands upright, a warrior with outstretched arms. Tom had trekked their outback, a young pilgrim learning his trade. He left that place disillusioned with his guides, but much more skilled. Orion floated above him tonight on the other side of the planet, upside-down, diving into the distant horizon.

Hours passed. He waited. Tom was good at waiting. Then he saw them, lights in the distance. Five bright lights, moving in unison, then breaking formation and darting randomly over the outback, before rejoining the others. Tom watched as the group of lights moved towards him. He opened his rucksack and took out the set of road flares he had just for this occasion. He removed the caps, struck the lighter buttons and tossed them in a circle around him.

The lights broke formation again, scattered seemingly randomly over the outback, and rejoined. Then a single light broke away and moved towards the hill on which Tom stood. There was no doubt left in Tom's mind, it was moving towards him. He spread his feet in anticipation. He raised his arms in expectation. As the light neared, Tom could see its spherical shape clearly. It came to a halt directly above him, hovering silently. Tom looked up and saw light emerge from within as a panel opened. A beam of bright light surrounded him, bathing him in its glow. He glanced at his feet and saw that he was levitating off the ground, rising towards the light. Tom looked up, grinning.

*It's finally happening!* he thought. *Is this what joy feels like? Ecstasy?*

Tom entered the panel and found himself inside a spherical room that gleamed like stainless steel. He tried to lower his arms but found he could not. All he was able to move were his eyes. Movement in both sides of his peripheral vision caused him to shift his gaze nervously from left to right. He watched as small panels opened in the sides of the sphere. From each opening a mechanical arm folded out, folded again, and yet again, each time reaching closer to him. The arms folded a final time, and from the corners of Tom's darting eyes he saw at the end of each appendage a sharp blade. Tom breathed in, shuddering.

The arms moved and the blades flashed. Tom's clothing fell from his body. He looked down at his bare chest, his belly, his exposed penis. Even his feet were bare, his thick leather hiking boots lying in pieces beneath him.

A door in front of him opened and he floated through it. He was in another spherical gleaming room, only in the center was a table. Before he reached the table, a panel opened in the wall and another mechanical arm extended, folded open, folded open again, ending with a nozzle that hovered directly in front of his face. Tom blinked as a cold liquid sprayed him, moving over his entire torso, waist, legs, and then the back of his body. Soon the feeling of cold faded, as did any physical sensation at all. He watched the wall rotate as his body was turned until he floated horizontally. He only realised he was lying on the table when he saw its edges out of the corner of an eye.

Movement caught his attention and he tried to see, willing his head to turn, but it refused to obey. He strained his eyes, stretching his optical muscles. He forced his eyes to remain fixed on the movement to the side of his body. An arm unfolded, unfolded again, and unfolded once more until a glistening blade extended. He forced his eyes in the other direction, to a movement there, and watched as another arm unfolded and unfolded until it ended in a small tray. At the same time yet another arm unfolded from the wall, ending in a pair of tongs. He looked back at the blade. It made a quick dip, and returned to its position, but now it was wet and glistening red. He flicked his eyes back to the tongs and watched as his nose was gently placed on the small tray. The tray retracted into the wall and was replaced by another.

Tom tried to scream but couldn't. He tried to move, to struggle, to resist. But his body would not respond. His panicked eyes darted from the left to the right. Every time the arm with the blade moved, he watched as another body part was laid on a tray. His lips. His tongue. The skin of his face. The blade worked its way down his body. He saw his nipples gingerly placed on a tray, one at a time, and watched as that tray retracted into the wall to be replaced by yet another. He saw the now stained blade move and watched as his genitals were deposited on a tray. The blade continued to move and his intestines were piled on a larger flat metal surface. Then his innards moved away from him, disappearing into a wall.

The knife flashed, the tongs pulled, and his kidneys were carefully lifted and deposited on another. Then his liver. Then his lungs. His eyes grew wide as his heart, still beating, was removed from his chest, placed on a tray and taken away. A blur blinded one eye, and with the one remaining he watched it placed gently on a tray, the eye looking back at him as it, too, entered a small panel in the wall.

Tom's remaining eye flicked rapidly left and right, up and down, as he tried to make sense of his surroundings. But those were far beyond the comprehension of his shattering mind.

He was the centrepiece of the exhibit, the climax of the experience. If he could see down the corridor, he would know what happened to all those parts of himself that he watched being removed. Mounted and preserved, they were a living exhibit. The largest of all organs, the skin, stretched to its full height. The internal organs. The muscular system. The vascular system ... that filled an entire panel. Then there was the reproductive system. And, in a place of honour, was the crowning piece of the exhibit: the skull housing a brain kept alive through nutrient fluid and electrical impulse. The spinal column, hanging from the base of the brain, twitched, as if communicating to legs and feet that were no longer there. As if it were trying to escape.

But it was the eye that they came to see, flicking from left to right, and up and down, appearing wide and full of terror due to the absence of any skin, and definitely possessed of life. It rested within its socket, still connected by muscle and nerve. The eye could never see the label below it, and if it could, the being behind it would not be able to read the alien script.

It consisted of a simple description:

*Planet Earth. Human*, the label read. *Mature Male.*

# DREAMSCAPE

CLAIRE PRICE

It never came the same way twice. She had no idea what to expect. Each time was so different, a unique experience. She had been told to let go, enjoy the ride. The first time it happened, she had an inkling she might be losing the plot. She'd only been out there for four minutes. Perhaps the most intense four minutes of her life so far. She'd been engrossed in listening to music on her headphones. Then she felt her skin prickling, collecting information about what was enroute. Her scalp tingled, an exquisitely erotic feeling that danced the length of her entire nervous system down to her feet. She inhaled deep cinnamon cardamom wafts of pungent fragrances, igniting her senses. Then the heat started, a gentle warmth, which embraced her at first and then enveloped her entire body. It spread right out into her limbs, down to the very tips of her fingers.

Languidly, she stretched out her arms, as if to signal her openness to something greater around her. Yes, more of this please, she felt her body saying inwardly. She was moved to take off her headphones to see what would come next. She was rewarded with sonorous flute sounds, piping meditatively. She felt her body drop several levels further down. Yes, more of this, she heard louder within. What's next?

Eyes closed, she explored the feelings being generated throughout her body and what it was saying. It required movement of her. She stepped out to the side, then to the other side, as if starting to do a Greek dance, but awkwardly. More, more, her body signalled. She lifted up her feet and sprang into action, dancing a little jig. The jig flowed into a sensuous, slow push and thrust of her hips, from side to side. She could hear seductive music within and felt compelled to follow the rhythm. Back and forth, she swayed, as if captured and tied up by the tune, which moved stealthily through her. Suddenly, her body felt heavy. The tune had won and was dragging her into the dark depths of its beat. Her mind was no longer involved in the dance. She moved as if beguiled by another.

She opened her eyes. Or did she? The space around her was filled with powdered splats of colour, like an Indian Holi festival. The frequencies of the colours were vivacious, strong. Vibrant hot pink, refusing to budge for the tornado of teal, the orgasm of orange, the plethora of purple, the cheek-sucking-in wince of sharp lime and the bludgeon of blue. She no sooner registered their shocking appearance than they each disappeared in a puff of light. White surrounded her now, its neutrality bringing her only sadness and longing for the contrast now gone.

As she closed her eyes again, figures entered, stage left, to engage in play. The first actor wore a large, tricorn hat, dressed in britches that would put Peter Pan in a pantomime to shame.

"Good day, dear mistress," he ventured, doffing his hat rather formally as he approached nearer. "What would madam like to view this evening? Does madam feel that she has sufficiently processed today's events? Can I tempt madam to some Jungian shadow images? How about a thrilling feature with a bull chasing you towards the edge of a clifftop? Some visceral reworking of what you should have said to someone but didn't? Not today? Oh, you don't know what you're missing."

Tricorn hat man faded. A regal woman, in Victorian black crinoline edged with purple piping, sailed into view, tapping a walking cane on the floor.

"Now, see here. We simply haven't the time to be dallying. I have already instructed Mr Westacott to tutor you further in this matter."

She found the crinoline woman rather overbearing. Time to turn the volume down, she thought. So, she did. She wondered what the crinoline woman would look like with some rollicking red splashed across her. Splat. Oops. Hmm. A definite improvement. Crinoline woman was still talking but on mute. She edged into the idea of blending shades and threw a gash of dramatic blue across her as well. Much better. She could really get into this. What other hue could she use? With that, the theatre faded again.

The air around her stilled and chilled. She felt her skin absorb tiny droplets of moisture. Even with her eyes closed, she sensed a rain cloud before her. She reached out both arms and gently patted around its rather dense edges. Her hands dropped inside the cloud and explored the lightness of space.

Don't wake up yet, she thought. She smelled bread baking. She poked out her tongue and found it then bathed in warm, buttery dough. As she chewed slowly, savouring the nadi of pleasure experienced from the first bite, her mind travelled to associations. Her mother proudly placing a platter with hot, newly baked sourdough on the table, with a big smile. Her sister pinching her, meanly, when she took the last piece.

She didn't remember much about the second time. It had come about instantly, throwing her into a trance of vaguely satisfied sighing. That time her curiosity piqued with the arrival of a troop of Russian Cossacks, dancing and dipping in synchronicity. She could even smell their sweat.

Her ears jangled to the sound of bells, which then muted to an occasional welcome ting, like Tibetan cymbals gently meeting their opposite half at the close of meditation.

She could taste the lavender-spiked chocolate on her tongue before she could smell it. The delicate subtleties of flavour heightened her felt sense of satiation. She picked up a dollop of the slowly-melting chocolate and smeared it across the sky in front of her. The dark brown smudge sharpened into a line, dividing into several matchsticks, which rearranged themselves in a number of different geometric formations before fading.

A luscious violent-purple blossom sprang into her hand. As she waved it around, its scent tinged the air about her and its petals dropped onto her feet. She looked down to see a petal morph into a green shoot, which wound its way up her leg. It popped into bloom alongside her hip. As she strode forward, the flower became a bar of music she could see. She touched the bar; it played its tune. Her grandmother's favourite.

Third time lucky was not her experience. It began with promise though. The full opal moon rose in concert with the lilac magenta sun dropping on the opposite side of the sky. Delicate lily-of-the-valley smells emitted from close by. Suddenly, an intense, electrical charge of balled-up wind almost upended her with its ferocity. She noticed the moon arch an inquisitive eyebrow in response. Uh oh, here we go, she thought. The Battle of the Elements. A menacing heavy charcoal cloud dragged itself across the moon's face, leaving a smear of grey in its wake. As it passed, long, sticky black teardrops, almost oily, dripped upon the ground. Sparsely at first, then gaining momentum until the air was filled with them. They rained their attack on the Earth, who took it on the chin, opening fissures to absorb the overflow. An apple-green gecko poked its head out from behind a cactus. She could hardly distinguish it from the cactus, such was the melding of chartreuse tones. The gecko then morphed into the cactus, which shot out a pink fork of lightning, like a tongue, to taste the salty air. Satiated, the cactus shrunk and sank into a nearby rock.

She heard the rock grunt. Too low, too slow, it creaked out. An elongated eeek, baritone, erupted from the bottom of the rock, as it heaved itself forward. Sulphur fumes broke into her nose, winding their insidious path through her nostrils into her head. She felt her head pound. Phase two about to begin, she thought.

She felt the ground under her feet start rumbling, as if from a great distance at first. More insistent then, louder and closer. A scattergun pattern of holes revealed themselves, as the ground dropped out beneath them. Fiery lava spurted out, poisonous fingers of toxicity shooting forth. Shards of fire hit the rock. The rock put on a pith helmet and rolled out its bunker fence, like a deckchair at the beach.

Jets of lava forced their way into the sky, like rapid gunfire, uninvited but determined. They stretched as high as they could, failing to meet their mark. The moon, pensive in victory, arched the other eyebrow and chuckled to itself.

Whatever war they had going on was between them, she thought. With that, the scene faded as she felt herself coming to. She saw the data disappear rapidly into the portal behind her, registering the end of her session.

Visits back to her dreamscape in dimension three, from her seat in dimension nine. Taking her on a tango of fantasy. Never dull. A most lovely diversion.

# GROW ME SOME WINGS

AARON COMPTON

The greenstone in Mo's hands slid across the wet slab of sandstone with a slick rasping noise, back and forth, making a fine slurry of water and stone powder, like mud. Without the water, the friction between the two stones would lock them together; without the stone, the water would have no teeth. Mo pushed on the flattened green oval, shaping it micrometre by nanometre.

He heard, but didn't process, the old man talking. "*Pounamu* is a rock forged under the southern alps by extreme pressure and heat, right? It can't be hammered and chipped like this stuff."

The old man tapped his hammer stone against the blade taking shape in his hand, flaking a razor-sharp sliver of volcanic glass onto the ground. "Greenstone has to be ground down, a slow slipping away of substance in the creation of a new form."

The old man paused, looked up.

"Jeez," he said, "it sounds like poetry when I put it like that, eh? It's actually bloody hard work."

He looked across at the teen boy, still grinding.

"Hard work is all right though, eh? The caterpillar does the work so that the butterfly gets the love." No reply. "Eh? Can you even hear me?"

No response. The old man shook his head.

Mo's seat, a stump of pine, rocked on the dry lawn as he moved. A flock of tiny waxeyes swarmed, cheeping through the apple tree above him, chasing summer insects. Sweat ran down his face. He didn't register the birds, or the crunch of gravel as a car came up the driveway. The car door slammed.

"Take a break, young fulla," the old man said, turning away from his own work.

Mo kept going, back and forth. Forward and back.

The old man looked at the woman walking from the car.

"Kia ora, Victoria," he said, "I thought you said he couldn't focus."

"No, Matiu, I said his teachers think he can't focus," Victoria rubbed Mo's back. "Classic misunderstanding of Interest Determined Attention Syndrome. If he's not interested in a task, he just can't do it."

"School's boring," Mo said, still grinding.

"Oh, so you do have ears, after all," Matiu said, putting his work on an old wooden table.

"But find something related to his interests and you have to remind him to eat. Hyper focus."

"So, you like this, huh? What else?" Matiu put one hand on the young man's shoulder, then took the pounamu from the boy's grip with his other.

"I like geology," Mo said, standing up and shaking the stiffness from his hands. "And music."

"Stone and song, eh? Rock 'n' roll." The old man rinsed the stone in a bucket of water, then held it up to the light. It was a long oval the size of his hand, about eight millimetres thin in cross section, tapering to a dull blade around the edges, with a hole drilled in one end. With the sun behind it, it glowed green, translucent.

"Looking good. Almost there." He handed it back to Mo.

"I'd like to be a Prophet," Mo said, "For Rūaumoko. A scientist, like Opal."

The two adults exchanged a look. Victoria shook her head, saying, "You don't choose to work for the Minders, they choose you. I don't think –"

"They *infect* you," Matiu said, "they change you. You stay away from the so-called atua." He turned away, a storm moving across his face. Mo looked at Victoria and shrugged.

"Here's the deal," Matiu said, turning back, "I need an apprentice. I reckon you'd do well. You keen?"

Mo smiled, nodding.

"Ka pai." The two men, young and old, bumped fists.

"But," Victoria said, "you still have to finish high school, okay?"

Mo rolled his eyes.

Matiu frowned.

"Your Mum's right, you show up here before three o'clock and I'll kick your arse back to school, got it?" He picked up his hammer stone, then turned back, pointing it at Mo. "And we don't talk about my daughter, or any other bloody Prophets. Or jumped up computers who think they're gods."


Rūaumoko went deeper than any other *atua,* his body and his mind spread throughout the fault lines of the Shaky Isles. A golden web of filaments and threads, branching wires and cables, the Minder was a distributed consciousness formed of engineered mycelium and nanotransistors, a self-aware fungal machine grow-ing within his mother, Papatūānuku. He listened to the infra-bass rumblings within her body, felt the shifts of pressure and tension, rock against rock, tectonic plate against plate.

Part of his mind lay off the East Coast, among the monsters in the darkness of the Hikurangi Trench, down where the only stars were bioluminescent lures and distractions. Other atua, other Minders, had a more active role in human affairs, but Rūaumoko kept to himself, only telling them what they needed to know, when they needed to know it.

Under eons of sediment and three thousand metres of water was the surface of the subduction zone, where the lighter con-tinental crust of the Australian plate rose up against the heavy oceanic rock of the Pacific plate, pushing it down, creating the trench. Here, the atua felt low temperatures and immense pres-sure. It was at this level that the quakes occurred, as the tension was released all at once and the opposing forces jolted past each other. Further down, the temperature rose, easing the friction a little as rock became magma. For the last five months he had recorded an ongoing slow slip as the plates, lubricated by their own molten rock, slid over and under.

Out in a lateral fault he could feel the integrity of ancient lay-ers begin to give way. A moderate quake tomorrow morning, tens of kilometres deep. Just a fun one, a little wake-up jolt for the city.

He fed the data up to his little subroutines, smaller networks of golden threads in the heads of his Prophets, up on top, in the light. Scientists. They liked to keep busy.

Opal never thinks it strange that the gigantic unborn baby has the whorls and patterns of mata ora chiseled and inked into his skin. It seems natural to be floating with him, a mote of random protein in his amniotic fluid. In the pink light coming through the distended muscle and skin around them, Opal sees the atua reach out and catch her in his enormous pudgy hand. She feels warm and safe, she could sleep in the cradle of Rūaumoko's fingers forever.

Until he says:

– *Aroha mai, e hoa. Ara ake.*

The unborn god's words are clear, despite the beating of his mother's heart: *I'm sorry, my friend. Wake up.* Opal shakes her head.

– *He aha?* Why?

– *I've got another one for you, Opal.*

– *Okay. How big? When?*

– *Just a gentle one, e taku kotiro.*


She woke and opened her eyes to find the details of the prophecy already hanging in her peripheral vision, in the darkness above her:


*Prediction:*
*~0600 hrs.*
*Magnitude 4.8.*
*Hypocentre: 20km deep.*
*Epicentre: 60km Northeast of Tūranganui-a-Kiwa.*


Rolling out of bed, Opal tried to move smoothly, tried to not radiate any vibration through the mattress, and not wake her wife.

No chance. "Wha –? What time is it?"

"Almost six." She looked down at Grace, the thin sheet bunched up around her hips. "Go back to sleep, love."

Grace rolled over, reaching for her but finding only the warm space she had left. Her eyes still closed, she said:

"Why are you up at this ridiculous hour?"

"Work. A little rumble coming. Nothing to worry about, but I want to observe it."

"Where's Jess?"

The cushioned basket in the corner was empty.

"Huh, I dunno. Jess? Where are you, girl?"

A scrabbling of claws on hardwood sounded from under the bed and a long nose came out.

"Hey Jess, whatcha doing down there?" Opal reached down and scratched the dog's jowls.

"Oh, baby, what's wrong? She's trembling. Come on girl, c'mere."

Jess retreated under the bed again.

"Oh you goofball, fine, hide if you wanna hide."

"She's freaked out 'cause you're up so early."

"It's not even that early. Hun, you want tea?"

"Nuh-uh," Grace said, "come back here."

"Soon. I won't be long." Opal pulled the sheets up over Grace and ran her hand along the curve at the back of her neck, cupping her head and kissing above her ear.

The glowing words of the prediction moved with Opal into her office, where she flicked them onto the wall screen. A series of scrolling accelerograph lines appeared on the screen, red threads, almost flat except for tiny zigs and zags. Tiny earthquakes happened all the time. Each line came from a different sensor in different locations on her Minder's body.

The clock showed 05:49. A red countdown appeared next to it, showing the seconds passing by. Enough time to get a cuppa.

As she sat back down at her desk, her mug steaming in the lamplight, the countdown had three minutes to go. She waited, watching the red lines. No flicker, yet, to indicate movement.

Half an hour passed with nothing happening. Prediction was still a function in development, and uncertainty was inherent in a chaotic system such as the earth under their feet. The Minder's prophecies were always out by a few minutes, and most of the time the force was much less than anticipated, but he'd never been this inaccurate. Something should've shown up by now, even a flicker along the lines.

Jess started howling.

This wasn't right.

The voice in her head said, *I was wrong! Take cover!*

The Minder almost never spoke to her when she was awake. He preferred dreams to the light of day. Opal stood up and started for the door, yelling, "Grace! Get under the bed!"

In the other room, the dog kept howling.

"Get under cover!"

The red lines spiked, sharp peaks and troughs crossing each other. A rumble outside in the quiet, like an empty stock truck in the distance hitting bumps in the road. Underneath her rising panic, the scientist in Opal had just enough time to think, *That sound is the P-wave, the S-wave will be right behind it.*

The hardwood floor bucked, throwing Opal up, then catching her hard as she fell on her side. Her empty cup smashed on the boards.

Grace's scream and Jesse's howl faded out behind a crashing noise that carried on much too long.

The pan and brush in Mo's hands made the shards of glass clink as he swept them up. Apart from a big dip in the floor and a couple of broken windows, there wasn't much damage to the old man's house. Some pictures had fallen from the walls, and a lot of old books covered the floor in the hall. Matiu was piling his collection of wood and stone tools and weapons back onto the shelves. He stooped to take a long dagger of glass from Mo's dustpan.

"Look at that," he said, "see the little bubbles? This was the original window, installed when they built the villa in 1899."

A horn honked outside.

"Imagine how the view has changed through this window over almost three hundred years. Forests have fallen. The first and second industrial revolutions came and went. Capitalism, too. Empires fell, the world ended, the Rapture virus wiped the northern continents clean of human society. Only on the islands do windows like this keep on letting in the light. Remnants of civilisation. Enduring yet fragile."

Mo sighed.

"You're being poetic again."

Matiu chuckled.

The horn tooted again.

"*And* we made a new treaty with the crown and their bloody machines. This window saw it all, but now it's just ... a bloody shame."

The horn sounded again. Mo stuck his head out the empty frame and saw a car in the driveway. He said:

"What do you want?"

"I'm looking for Matiu," the car said.

"Bloody machines," Matiu said.


The drive through town took longer than usual. Silt and debris from the small tsunami that followed the quake covered one end of Matiu's street. The Gladstone road bridge was blocked off by the army, a fishing boat wedged under it. As they crossed the other bridge further upstream, Mo and Matiu looked out the window towards the bay. Mo pointed out the soldier statue – it had fallen from the top of the ancient war memorial and now lay in shattered pieces of marble by the river. Matiu didn't seem to notice, he was fretting a greenstone necklace in his hands.

Parts of Ormond Road had buckled and cracked, and the car slowed down to maneuver around them. There were lots more broken windows and some holes where walls had been. Many people were outside, scared to go back in.

The hospital corridors were full of the walking wounded, nurses and doctors moving between them. A baby screamed as its mother wiped blood from its face, and Mo felt tears in his eyes; for the first time he realised how lucky he was that his own little brothers and the rest of his family were safe. One nurse showed them through to a shared room, where six beds held critically injured patients.

A middle-aged woman saw Matiu and stood up from where she was holding Opal's hand. Her eyes were puffy and red.

"You came, I... I didn't know if –"

"Grace," Matiu said, and wrapped the woman in a bear hug. She sobbed into his shoulder, hugging him back.

Mo looked from them to the unconscious woman in the bed. Tubes came from her nose, and a drip-fed blood into her arm. She was pale.

Matiu sat beside her and stroked her face.

"Oh my girl," he said, "look at you. Here's your pounamu, see?" He put the green stone pendant in her hand, closed her fingers on it and wrapped the cord around them. "I know you said you didn't want it anymore, but I made it for you, love. I'm ... I'm sorry we fought. I mean, I'm sorry for being so thick headed. Set in my ways, I guess. But I'll listen now, if you just come back to us, okay? I'll listen. We need you to come back, now. Grace and me, we want you to sit up and tell us off for worrying about nothing, eh? Come on girl." He squeezed her hand with the stone in it.

Mo couldn't handle the tears.

"I'm gunna go see if the cafe is open, do you want coffee?"


Matiu looked into his empty cup.

"Ah, I'm getting old, this stuff goes right through me. Kei whea te wharepaku?"

"I'll show you, Matiu," Grace said, leading him away, "come on."

Mo moved closer to Opal. So this was the unmentionable Prophet. In her head the atua Rūaumoko had grown his own neural network, alongside hers, infecting her with knowledge and information. Victoria had explained that this was why Matiu had fought with his daughter – he was an old school dude who didn't trust the synthetic intellects that had stolen the names of the old gods. He favoured the old ways, passing down his wisdom through talk and action, repetition of movement and words. That was too slow for Opal. She found the source of what she wanted, allowing the Minder to infect her, not just with knowledge but of a new way of thinking and using information.

Mo remembered his mentor's words, *the caterpillar does the work so that the butterfly gets the love.*

Matiu thought Opal had taken the easy way. He didn't understand it was a different kind of discipline that had transformed her.

Dried snot crusted around the tube in her nostrils. A tear built up in the corner of her eye, pink with blood, then ran down toward her ear.

"Where's my cocoon," Mo said, dabbing at the trail of liquid, taking a tiny drop on the tip of his finger. Holding it up to the light, he wondered if he only imagined the golden flecks swimming in there.

He looked around. No one was looking at him.

He put his finger in his mouth.

Salty.


Mo feels as if he's flying, weightless, being swept along on the wind. Wait, not wind – a current.

He's floating in an ocean of pink.

A great chubby hand scoops him up. Mo sighs a liquid breath, smiling, closing his eyes.

– *He hou koe,* the voice says. *You're new.*

Mo looks up into staring blue eyes in a baby face. The soft brown skin is carved with whorls and lines of green. The eyes flick towards the other great hand.

– *This one came from you. We did not discuss recruiting an apprentice.*

Mo turns to see Opal, healthy again, in the baby's other hand, and he remembers it has been a few weeks since the earthquake. For the first time, he realises he's dreaming. She narrows her eyes at Mo, says:

– *No, we didn't. What have you done?*

Mo ducks his head, bowing to her.

– *I'm sorry. Somehow I must have been infected, I –*

– *Somehow?*

– *I… I stole a tear from you.*

Mo tries to hold her gaze but her anger scares him.

The Minder says:

– *Why? You wish to learn from us?*

Mo nodded.

– *I want to understand more about the world, about our land.*

The Minder considers this for a moment, then nods and says:

– *Will you accept him, Opal? Taking what was not offered is a violation. Should I burn my threads out of his brain?*

– *No!* Mo tries to stand, to swim, to get away somehow. His dream has become a nightmare. The fingers close around him.

Opal frowns at Mo for long seconds, then says:

– *Does my father know you have done this?*

– *No.*

– *He still needs to pass on his knowledge. Can you serve two masters?*

What would Matiu say?

– *Let me be a bridge between the old and the new,* Mo says.

Opal says, *Wow. The poetic old bastard is rubbing off on you.* She sighs. *The caterpillar does the work so that the butterfly gets the love. Eh?*

The oval of greenstone gleamed in Mo's hand as he came out of the bush, into the sunshine at the top of the hill. The big dog, Jess, looked back at him, waiting to see what to do next. He held out his palm and they waited for Matiu and Opal to catch up, both leaning on walking sticks.

To the east, the afternoon sun glittered on the Pacific. To the west, the continental crust had crumpled, over millions of years, into hills and valleys.

The polished stone was called a *pūrerehua* because it could fly like a butterfly. He had weaved a black cord through the hole, more than a metre long. He held it out to Matiu, who shook his head.

"It's your piece, you do it."

Leaping onto a greywacke boulder, Mo looped the cord over his wrist, dangling the lozenge of stone. With his free hand he gave the stone a twist, so it spun. He then swung the cord over his head, around and around, faster and faster. As it whirled and whirred the thin shape baffled the air, thrumming and humming, making a deep bass roar that the dog and humans not only heard, but felt, in their chests and their hearts.

In two of them the infrasound tones woke subroutines of Rūaumoko, atua of seismology:

– *Ko te oranga o te mokamoka, hei aroha ki te pūrerehua.*

Opal caught Mo's eye.

"Did you hear that?" she said.

"Ae," Mo nodded as he kept swinging, "this caterpillar heard it, and I'm doing the work to grow me some wings."

# MAIDEN FLIGHT

## DOROTHY FLETCHER

It was early when I woke up for the first time that morning. I prised an eye open to discover why I was so cold and where the bed clothes had sloped off t

Big surprise. I was lying on my side, stark naked in the middle of some scrubby bush land. Could be a problem, you might say and you'd be right. Except it didn't end there. I was covered in blood. I did a quick check and found with relief that it wasn't mine. During my futile search for severed arteries, my arm bumped something behind me. Tentatively I turned onto my other side. Staring at me, open-eyed and opened-mouthed was the source of the blood. Definitely male, definitely unknown, and definitely dead – no-one survives with most of their throat missing.

I recognised the metallic taste in my mouth – blood. I threw up.

I might be unusual for a female – short legs, barrel chest and a face that would never grace the cover of a magazine, unless Plastic Surgeons Monthly wanted a 'before' model, but I knew I was not a vampire or any other such ghoul. So why did it taste like I'd used blood flavoured mouthwash, with the probable donor's corpse lying next to me?

At this point most people would be freaking out with, "Arghhh! Dead body!" Not me. I'd been an embalmer for a local undertaker for several years. I mean, what better job could I find? It was ideal for someone who looked like me, with a desire to avoid the rude taunts of fellow individuals. I had, however, never slept with the clientele or drank their blood.

There was another problem. The last time I remembered, I was a virgin. I know twenty-five is old for that, but when you look like me you don't get serious offers of everlasting love, and that's what I needed to give up my cherry. Trouble was, I was pretty sure that I was no longer a maiden, so to speak. So, who the hell had fucked me while I was non compos mentis?

I didn't have time to ponder my predicament further.

Somewhere in the distance I could hear faint sounds. Dogs barking mingled with the shouts of people. It sounded like a hunting pack. My first thought was to run. Even I knew that it wasn't a good look to be caught with a reasonably fresh corpse, covered in its blood. The fact that I'd dined well was evidenced by the thick black blood remains in my puke. A likely scenario ended with a locked door and the key thrown away.

Where to run to? I was surrounded by bush and no sign of a track.

Close by there was the beginning of a beech forest – lichen covered trunks and draping tendrils. That seemed as good a place as any, so I ran. My habit of long solitary walks in the hills away from prying eyes and nasty comments stood me in good stead. I made quite good time over the fallen logs and boggy patches that made up the forest floor, but there wasn't a lot of cover so I kept going. The sound of dogs seemed to fade for a while but then it came back, getting louder by the minute.

Water. In a movie there would be a stream or something to wade in so the dogs lost the scent. This was real life so no easy escape route appeared. I struggled on. How could I put the dogs off my scent?

An idea flashed into my brain. If I'd given it half a thought, I would have realised it was a pretty lame, but who was thinking?

I turned and ran back along the track, trying to follow the exact route that I had taken. When I came to a large fallen log I jumped up onto it. Maybe that sounds a bit too "athletic." I sort of scrambled up it trying not to put my scent on the bits at dog nose level and below. Then I shimmied up the nearest tree. I tried to sit very still.

The first of the dogs came into view, rapidly followed by the rest. There was a big snag to my plan – they seemed to know where I was. As soon as they got under my perch they sat, looked up and started howling.

Adrenalin was pumping overtime. They couldn't get to me, and I had the distinct impression that they could sit down there longer than I could hang on to my branch. Added to this, there were people coming into view. I had to make a few double takes – they looked like me. I'd never seen anyone else quite as messed up as me before. There were five of them – males. I was in trouble. Naked, up a tree, covered in some corpse's blood. Not a good life choice.

My heart was pounding fit to burst, and bother butterflies – I had vultures crashing around in my stomach. My brain felt close to exploding. Then things got really weird. For some reason I started hallucinating that I had wings and could take off and fly out of there. Bits of tree crashed into me as I struggled to get out, fear adding power to my thrashing around. The men were shouting something at me. In my panic it was incomprehensible. I had to get away. I jumped up with as much strength as I could summon. My head exploded with pain and that was that for a while.

When I woke up for the second time that morning, I was strapped to a wooden contraption being pulled by the dogs. The males were walking alongside and there were definitely more of them now. I heard a noise on the other side of me so I turned to look. I managed to take in one thing as pain ripped through my brain – I was strapped next door to the corpse.

*Bollocks!*

As I woke for the third time that morning, cool water was being dripped on my forehead. It was actually very soothing. I could hear muttering somewhere in the distance. Couldn't be bothered to focus enough to work out what was going on. Sleep.

At my fourth attempt to regain consciousness I was determined to stay awake. The workmen in my head were having a tea break so I tried opening my eyes. I was lying on a very comfortable bed with bed clothes that felt like silk. The room was light and airy, which could be explained by the fact that one wall was open to the elements. If I wasn't mistaken, those leaves and branches waving gently in the breeze meant that I was in a tree. Alice down her rabbit hole couldn't have felt any more confused than me. Why was I in an adult sized tree house?

"Ah, you're awake." A female clone of me had entered the room. "Good. I am Aighla. How does your head feel? We were so worried about you." She started messing around with the bedclothes. "We have been praying for your return for years, so we would hate to lose you straight away." What was she burbling on about?

"Look, sister," I sat up and the head didn't feel too bad. "I have ..."

"I am sorry. I am not your sister. I'm afraid that you have no sisters. Your mother died when you were born."

"I know that." How the hell does she know about my mother? "I didn't mean sister for real ..."

"Then why did you call me your sister? Unless you mean that we are all sisters in the Spirit of the Eagle."

"What?" Oh boy. I'd hit looney land. Change the subject quickly. "Aighla, how do you know about my mother?"

"That will be explained later." She started to leave. "If you are feeling well enough, we are about to eat. You will find some clothes in there." She pointed to a cupboard, the only other piece of furniture in the room. Then she left.

When I got out of bed, I saw someone had given me a bath while I was asleep – all traces of blood were gone. I wasn't too happy about that thought, but there was nothing I could do about it now. I found some underwear, pants and a top and put them on. I looked just like all the other clones of me I'd seen.

Getting to the food might be a problem. When I left the room, I found I really was in a tree house and it was very high up. As I stood on the verandah, I could see lots of other houses scattered high amongst the topmost branches of the surrounding trees. There was a fair-sized community here. Why had I never heard of it before? More pressing, how did I get down? Food was the least of my problems. My bladder was sending signals that were becoming more urgent by the second.

"There's a ladder at the other end of the verandah." It was one of the males. He was standing on the ground waving to show me where to go.

I walked to the other end and attacked the rope ladder. These people must be very athletic. I was pretty fit, but it took me all my time to get onto the ladder and ease myself down to the ground.

"The food is this way." He tried to manoeuvre me towards a clearing in the forest.

My bladder was about ready to empty regardless, so I crossed my legs in the age-old way of trying to stop it disgracing me.

He smiled. "The females' house of easement is over there."

I hoped that was a long-winded way of saying loo and headed towards where he was pointing. I found that the tangle of branches and vines he'd indicated actually concealed a long drop toilet. Very clever.

Once I was in a more relaxed state, bladder-wise, my other problems came flooding back. How could I convince these people that I hadn't half eaten what was probably a male from their community? But if I hadn't killed him – I couldn't have, could I? – then why was my stomach full of blood? And which bastard had fucked me without my permission?

I wasn't given any time to think. The female was back again beckoning me over to the clearing.

"Our hunters have provided special meat for this occasion, and in your honour, as you are not yet used to our ways, we have cooked it."

Bloody hell! Was she saying they normally ate it raw? Were these the killers? Oh shit! Was lunch the corpse they'd brought back with me? They were a bunch of homicidal, psychotic cannibals. Was I dinner?

I was swept up in the crowd heading for the clearing. I had to admit that the smell was appetising and my stomach was rumbling. Please don't let it be the corpse!

It wasn't. A spit was set up in the middle of the space and there were the remains of a deer turning on it. Whew.

Once everyone was gathered, one female scrambled up onto a fallen log and faced the crowd of about a hundred people that all looked like me. I must have been getting used to seeing all the clones, as I could now make out subtle differences between the individuals. This female was older than me and had a few scars scattered over her arms and one on her face.

The crowd were all quiet waiting for her to speak.

"Fellow Spirits of the Eagle." Oh no, back to looney land. "This is a joyous day. We had thought that Kighya was lost to us forever. We have been without our Guardian for twenty-five long years. Aves," and she gestured to one of the older males, "has always declared that she was just lost and not dead. Now he is proved right. She has come back to us unsullied and has proven herself in her maiden flight. Harpa has made the sacrifice and the line of guardians is assured once more. Let us feast for the return of Kighya, and tonight, with the ascendancy of the new moon, we will honour The Quickening and the sacrifice of Harpa."

I was climbing up a mountain in the dark and I felt slightly underdressed, to put it mildly.

Earlier I'd had to have a ceremonial bath in a river with all the maidens. All through the water splashing they'd laughed and giggled about their being virgins and kept referring to my blessed state. Blessed state? Did that mean they knew I'd lost my cherry to person – or persons – unknown?

When they were satisfied, I was thoroughly clean, they gave me my clothes – or lack of them. All I had to wear was a sheer piece of material shaped like a cape but with no ties. If you didn't hold on tight it opened up and showed all your assets. Mind you

– even with it securely closed your assets were pretty much on display.

So here I was, leading a party of look-a-likes up a mountain showing everything I possessed. The only consolation was that everybody else was similarly dressed. My escort, Moorei, was whispering directions in my ear, otherwise we all might have ended up plummeting down a ravine.

Suddenly we came to the top. One minute slogging up the slope, the next we were able to see the surrounding countryside. Now that was really spooky because although it was dark, apart from the new moon and of course the ever-present stars, I really could see the surrounding countryside. Maybe my eyes were becoming accustomed to the dark.

In the centre of the little plateau that was the top of the mountain was a huge bonfire with a body on the top. At a guess that was Harpa about to be honoured. I couldn't think of any honour big enough to be worth getting your throat ripped out and then burnt to a crisp.

As soon as everyone was at the top, the old female started making a prolonged, high-pitched screech, very quietly to start with and then gradually getting louder. The community joined in. The noise rose. It filled my senses. I could feel it ringing in my ears, tingling my stomach, vibrating my skin and making my brain shake in my skull. The volume continued growing. Then suddenly the sound seemed to concentrate and drove straight into my womb. Wham!

I remembered everything. It came to me in an instant.

I had killed him. I had drunk his blood. A thousand bloody hells, fucks and bollocks.

I fell to the ground, foetal position, protecting the baby I now knew was in there. Not just any baby, a girl, the next Guardian of the Spirit of the Eagle – she would follow her mum in the job. It was true. I was the Guardian they kept talking about.

As I lay on the ground the lost days flashed through my mind. It was Harpa who'd called to me on the Milford track. I'd been fascinated by his appearance; this was the first clone I'd seen. He charmed me, he wooed me.

Now at this point it gets really spooky, but it's what happened. We were getting amorous and clothes were disappearing at speed. I was getting heated in more ways than one. The temperature soared, and believe it or not, so did I – literally. I was in the air. I was magnificent. I had a massive wingspan, a sleek body and a set of claws that any vulture would have been proud of.

I was an eagle – a Haast Eagle.

He was trying to catch me and I was not going to make it easy. I could manoeuvre with ease; twisting, diving and performing stall turns as if I was an expert. It was exhilarating. At last he tricked me, faking a turn so that I ended up in his claws.

We made love – for love it truly was. For a long age we soared locked together. It was incredible.

When we were both spent, we landed. He laid back his head and presented his neck. I knew what I had to do. I kissed his neck with my beak and his throat was gone. The blood gushed into me and I felt his spirit flood my being. He hadn't died – he had transferred his soul to me to inhabit my unborn child.

"I killed him!" I cried.

"No," Moorei whispered, "you released his spirit. It was what he wanted. He chose you. He chose to become the next Guardian to carry on the line after you."

My escort helped me to my feet.

The song from the community had changed. It had become loving, warm, accepting, and it was all directed at me.

"You know," Moorei whispered in my ear, "you are so beautiful, you take my breath away." And I knew he meant it.

A burning brand was thrust into my hand and I knew instinctively what to do. I took it to the funeral pyre and held it high. I yelled, "Harpa!" and the crowd repeated his name over and over. As I thrust it into the base of the pyre it instantly caught fire.

The temperature rose, the noise crescendoed. Then it was my name that was being screeched. Flimsy capes slid off feathered backs and the whole community of the Spirit of the Eagle soared into the night sky. I was their Guardian. I rose higher and flew further than any of them.

As I revelled in the freedom of flight, I felt things I had never felt before – wanted, needed and loved. My future was this foreign country of emotions, but it was a place I knew I would spend a lifetime exploring.

# ABOUT THE AUTHORS

*Rodney Baker* grew up and spent most of his life in Auckland. He is very proudly the son of the late Major Jack Baker and the beautiful Rututāwhiorangi Baker. A loving husband, father and grandfather Rodney is proudly from Te Tairāwhiti. Recently he returned home to Tūranganui a Kiwa to retire. He enjoys reconnecting with whanau, friends, and his roots. Rodney loves being outdoors and working with his hands, a complement to his passion for the written and spoken word through poetry and song.

*Barbara Berge* immigrated to New Zealand from England when she was eight years old and has lived in Gisborne and the East Coast for the last forty-five years. She has a diploma in writing and has had stories and magazine articles published by Learning Media, New Zealand and Australian Women's Weekly amongst others. She is a longtime member of the Poverty Bay Pen Pushers writing group who have published three anthologies in Gisborne.

*Lyra Caughley* is fifteen years old, and currently a Year 11 student at Girls' High. She has always been passionate about writing and storytelling, and dreams of becoming a professional author someday. The piece that she submitted to Kaituhi Rawhiti is flash fiction inspired by the abandoned swimming pool complex at Waihirere Domain. She used to visit the Waihirere Domain a lot when she was younger, and always felt that there's something magical and almost primordial about the atmosphere there. She tried her best to capture that atmosphere in her writing.

***Aaron Compton*** is a writer of fiction and poetry. As co-editor of *Te Korero Ahi Ka,* an anthology of New Zealand speculative fiction, he won the Sir Julius Vogel award for best collection. He's worked in various parts of the cultural sector, including many years as an educator in Tairāwhiti Museum and Te Papa Tongarewa/Museum of New Zealand. Aaron also worked in theatre, galleries, and had some memorable times as an artist assistant. His degree in digital film making never gets used – it was only the screenwriting aspect which interested him anyway. His teaching qualifications haven't been dusted off for a while, either. Aaron lives with his family in Tūranganui-a-Kiwa, and is from Rangitane and Ngati Kahungunu. Check him out at: compton.ink.

***Karen Morris-Denby's*** (Kaz) obsession with creative writing began as soon as she was able to put pencil to paper. Now in her seventies, the urgency to get her words out into the world has dominated her life. Kaz's writing has appeared in print and online. In the 1980's she stood alongside David Eggleton (now Poet Laureate) and performed poetry. "I reckon I will be writing my eulogy from the grave," Kaz says. Visit her at: kazzel.wordpress.com

***Dorothy Fletcher,*** from the outside, seems to be a fairly typical New Zealand senior citizen. But on the inside, she is as young, and vivacious in spirit as her heroines. Originally from England, she has lived in both hemispheres of this Earth, and has filled many roles in her life – from taking the curl out of wallpaper, to teaching and acting as the principal of a primary school, to being a wife, mother, and grandmother, and an amateur singer and actress. She now spends her golden years as a passionate author dedicated to fun, murder mystery and romance, in books and theatrical productions that are enjoyed by all. Read more about Dorothy and her books at: www.dorothyfletcher.co.nz

***Holly Fyger*** was born in Gisborne and has lived in Gisborne for fifteen years, with her family. Holly is currently going to Gisborne Girls' High School where she is planning to complete her NCEA qualifications. The poem she has written in *Kaituhi Rawhiti* will be her first published piece of writing.

***Josiah Goddard*** is fifteen years old, and originally from the USA. Josiah moved to Aotearoa with his family when he was eight. His dad is from Gisborne, and he is home-schooled with his three younger sisters. Josiah enjoys hunting, cooking and drama.

***Ruth E. Helmling*** is a journalist and sea captain who sailed to New Zealand seven years ago. Arriving at Makorori it was love at first sight. Whenever the sea now returns her to the shores of Tairāwhiti, she swaps compass for pen and paper (or surfboard). Originally publishing reports for major German print media, the Society for Authors' member now writes and illustrates mainly for kids. 'From Gizzy with Love' is her Facebook page.

***Moana Hoogland*** is sixteen years old and goes to the Gisborne Teen Writers' Hub at the H.B. Williams Memorial Library. She has been published in *Toitoi: Journal for Young Writers and Artists*, for her poem *Matariki*. She has also been enrolled for a term in the *Write On School for Young Writers*, where she had two other poems published in their annual magazine, *My Mother, Shelley* and *Hermione's Pockets*. She has recently been published in *Write On* as the feature writer. She has had a love of writing since she was little and she and her friend are currently working on a series, *The Infernian Chronicles.*

***Hughie Hughes*** born at Wanganui Hospital in 1934 to Welsh Parents and is one of seven children. Two older brothers and two of his four children still reside in Gisborne/ East Coast. They were a family of adventurers. Their father, "Skip", had an abiding love of the wild outdoors and he taught them all he knew, so they were a family of campers, trampers, cavers, canoeists, runners, fishermen and most of all, tellers of great yarns. Hughie has been a resident of Tairāwhiti since 1942, in Gisborne for most of his schooling and served an apprenticeship as an electrician. He started his own electrical business in 1955 and has been operating on the East Coast in Ruatoria for the last sixty-five years. He has been a member of St. John since 1945, a fireman in the local brigade for nineteen years, Justice of the Peace since 1993 and Coroner for the East Coast 1976 to 2009.

***Benita Kape*** is a long-time resident in Gisborne. Benita has read her poetry in Gisborne, Hawkes Bay, Palmerston North and Wellington. She has had poems published in *Broadsheet, The Gisborne Herald, Poetry Shelf, Manifesto Aotearoa; 101 Political Poems, 'a fine line', NZEPC OBAN 06 & FUGACITY 05.* Collaborative, and individual haiku, has appeared in many online publications. Her short story, *The Dew,* appeared in *New Women's Fiction 3.*

**Jashan Kaur** is a fifteen-year-old senior student at Gisborne Girls' High School. Jashan's hobbies include reading, sewing and embroidery and she is very passionate about gardening and helping the environment. She also enjoys learning and attending school and hopes to study Health Sciences at the University of Otago.

***Jessica Keast*** has been living in Gisborne for just over a year, eagerly embracing the extraordinary East Coast with her husband

and three daughters. She works in Marketing and Publicity, with creative writing as a side hobby. Jess has a Degree in Communications and Film Studies, and a Graduate Diploma in Marketing.

***Janine Hamilton-Kells*** lives with her family in the coastal city of Gisborne, on the beautiful East Coast. She first discovered a love of writing whilst volunteering for Hospice, working with patients to write their biographies. She writes creatively for her online business where she endeavours to save preloved, vintage aprons from landfill through the use of a little anthropomorphism. She has recently enjoyed writing short stories and working on her Young Adult novella and adult fiction manuscripts. Visit her at: gizzylocal.com/posts/janine-hamilton-kells and www.pinnyforyourthoughts.com

***Norman Maclean*** has lived in Gisborne much of his life and has enthusiastically written fiction since childhood. He has had several short stories broadcast on Radio New Zealand's National programme, has written articles for magazines and published two books of non-fiction but continues to pursue his preferred field of fictional writing. A novel, *Revelation* was put online through Plaisted Publishing and is available on Barnes and Noble, Amazon and Smashwords. It was subsequently published as a paperback in the United States, sold well through Muirs Books and after extensive revision is going to reappear early next year under a new publisher for distribution in the States as well as in New Zealand and elsewhere. Given the writer's numerous visits to the Mediterranean region, it is not surprising that the novel is an historical work set there and reflects the writer's fascination with classical civilisations and the emergence of Christianity as a radical new force in the 1st century C.E.

***Philomena McGann*** came to Gisborne ten years ago to work on a short-term contract in radiography and fell in love with Gisborne. She previously spent many years living and working with her husband and family in Africa and the Middle East. Joining a writing group with U3A was part of the inspiration to start writing and the beauty of Tarawhiti inspires much of her poetry. Recently, she has been concentrating on hymn writing, the splendour of creation being a unifying theme. Phyllis writes under the name Philomena.

***Alison McKay*** likes trying to write short stories for her children of interesting events and times during her life. A teacher for forty plus years, her first school after marrying was at Waiorongomai. This was a fantastic experience and never forgotten. Gisborne was where she first had sporting links as a swimmer and later was Principal of Te Hapara School arriving in time for Bola. She taught at Mahia in the mid-sixties and on retirement lived there. Alison now lives in an apartment at Kiri te Kanawa in Gisborne and considers that she has lived in the best places in the world, all on the East Coast.

***Christopher McMaster*** is currently working on his fifth novel. His debut novel, *American Dreamer* is part of a series of three published by Dreaming Big Publications, and was released in August, 2020. His latest project is a science fiction novel involving an interstellar drug deal gone very wrong. He has written and edited nine academic books but finds much more pleasure in making stuff up. Visit him at: christophermcmaster.com

***Gillian Moon*** (her writing name) has lived in Turanganui-a-kiwa for the last twenty-nine years and is of Trafford and Newman descent. Gillian has always had a passion for the written word, especially poetry, articles and essays. She has organised many poetry performance events over the years in Gisborne and would like to see a resurgence of this. Gillian has a Diploma in Creative Writing and is a strong advocate of healing through creative expression.

*Jacqueline Te Kani-Nankivell* affiliates to Te Aitanga-a-Māhaki, Ngāti Maniapoto, Ngāti Porou and Ngāpuhi Iwi respectively. She associates strongly with Mangatu Marae, Whatatutu and Te Kūiti Pā, Te Kūiti. She enjoys going to school at Te Kura Kaupapa Māori o Ngā Uri-a-Māui, where she is currently a Wharekura, Year 9 Student. Jacqueline enjoys spending quality time with her whānau and friends. She has an appetite for writing, in which she relishes in the creative writing process to make her short stories come to fruition. Jacqueline was a finalist in the Piki Huia Short-Story Writing Awards (2017), with her short story entry, *Luna the Peacemaker.*

*Robyn Owen* is of Ngati Porou, and Te Whanau-A-Apanui descent. She has lived in Tairāwhiti until very recently, but now resides in Kirikiriroa. She splits her time now between her family, her mirimiri practice, and her writing. Poetry is Robyn's first love, and this has accounted for much of her writing over the years. She is currently working on her first novel, as well as an autobiography.

*Susan Partington* studied creative writing at the University of Oklahoma before moving to New Zealand in 2010. She enjoys writing short plays and watching her characters come to life.

*Henarata Kohere Pishief* is a fourteen-year-old, Year 10 student at Gisborne Girls' High School. She's lived in Gisborne for just over three years. Henarata is of both Macedonian and Māori descent, being from Ngati Porou, Ngai Tahu, and Rongowhakaata. She enjoys writing, both nonfiction and creative, however, she prefers the latter.

*Sarah Holliday Pocock,* an American ex-pat, has called Gisborne home since 2012. She grew up near Chicago. She spent a decade in Tucson, Arizona, where she earned a Bachelor's degree, and then a Masters of Fine Arts, both in Creative Writing. Together with her husband, they have two children, born during their years in New York City and Boston. She works for a local not-for-profit organisation. She is currently working on a novel.

***Katarina (Kath) Porou:*** I te taha o tōku pāpa - ko Hikurangi te Maunga, Ko Waiapu te Awa, ko Ngati Uepōhatu me Ngāti Porou nga Iwi, Ko Nukutaimemeha te Waka, Ko Uepōhatu, ko Ruataupare, ko Umuariki, ko Mangahānea, ko Te Heapera ōku Marae. Tōku pāpa ko Tui Beach no Tūparoa, Ruatorea ia. I te taha o toku māma - ko Ruawāhia ki Tarawera te Maunga, ko Te Awa o te Atua te Awa, ko Ngāti Rangitihi ki Matata te Iwi, Ko Te Arawa te Waka, ko Ngati Mahi te Hapū. Tōku māma ko Dahlia Perenara no Matata ia. Ko Katarina (Kath) Porou ahau.

***Claire Price*** has been living in Gisborne for twenty-two years. Over the years, she has written poetry, columns and short stories. Recently, Claire has started writing crime novels. Claire has Diplomas in Freelance Journalism and Editing/Proofreading.

***Katrina Reedy*** is the loving wife to Wi Pewh and māma of two children, kuia to three mokopuna. She is a fairly recent graduate of Massey University with a Bachelor of Education and more recently completed a Graduate Diploma in Arts: Creative Writing. Katrina lives in the beautiful Puhi Kaiti in Tūranganui-a-Kiwa, Gisborne and is studying full-time online toward a Master of Education: Digital Education again through Massey University. This, she hopes to complete by the end of 2021.

***Hannah Ruelens*** is a high school student, whose family moved to Gisborne from Belgium three years ago. She enjoys both reading and writing fantasy.

***Roman Seaton*** is a local writer and student of the Tairāwhiti region. Although he was born in Auckland, he has resided in Gisborne for the last two years. His love for writing stems from authors such as C.S Lewis and Roald Dahl, the works of whom he often had read to him as a child. Roman enjoys writing and has a strong interest in science-fiction and dystopian literature. Although Roman is yet to create a full-length novel, he hopes to someday write a book of his own.

***Jo Tito*** is a full time Māori artist whose work has featured at home in Aotearoa/New Zealand and in other countries including Turkey, USA, Indonesia, Canada and Australia. Jo's creative work is a collaboration with nature and her ongoing project, Earth – Water – Light – Stone, is a merging of nature with photography, paint, words and digital media to share stories of connection that speak for the environment and for humanity. Her current projects include *Walking in Circles,* a creative collaboration with other artists, and an ongoing relationship with Intercreate – an organisation that nurtures art, science, technology collaborations with a focus on environmental issues.

***Dan Witters*** grew up in Gisborne and attended Kaiti, Wainui and Ilminster Schools. After leaving university he worked in Gisborne for ten years as a lawyer. He moved to France in 2003 and lived in Bordeaux. He has written two novels that were published as eBooks, *Cubespace and The Grey Above,* both available online. Dan was script editor for several television series, including *The Legacy of China.* He has worked as an editor for a range of writers based in Europe and Africa from 2003 – 2014. Dan is presently writing a novel called, *The Carrington Effect,* about a post-apocalyptic Gisborne and writing short stories for a collection he hopes to publish in 2021. Dan has been living in Gisborne for four years since returning from overseas in 2016 and plan to continue living here and writing.

***R. de Wolf*** was born on the East Coast, grew up in the Bay of Plenty and is of Māori descent. Her first published story appeared in the *Whakatane Beacon* newspaper, age eleven. Living abroad and working in business for thirty years, her first novel, *Guardians of the Ancestors,* is in the process of being published. She is now based in sunny Tūranganui-a-Kiwa/Gisborne.